"SO, WHAT'S YOUR HANDLE, MISTER?"

Mosely's voice was vicious.

"Slocum, John Slocum."

There was a long pause, then Slocum saw something in their eyes. All three rose to their feet, their bodies tense. Slocum could hear the fire crackle, a coyote howl.

"Slocum," said Mosely, "your time has come."

The words were scarcely out of his mouth when Slocum's hand moved, a flash of lightning, his gun barking so fast it sounded like one shot.

Both Clem and Mosely had their guns out of their holsters, but only Mosely got off a shot, his bullet hitting the earth. They rocketed back, eyes wide with shock. They lay there dying, red blood pumping from their bodies, spreading over their shirts.

Clem turned painfully to Mosely and whispered, "You stupid bastard. I tole you we didn't need this. Now we'll never . . . get to . . . spend the money."

Mosely, whose strength was failing fast, muttered, "Only way to go, Clem. Bye." He shut his eyes.

JAKE LOGAN

SLOCUM'S DEBT

BERKLEY BOOKS, NEW YORK

SLOCUM'S DEBT

A Berkley Book/published by arrangement with
the author

PRINTING HISTORY
Berkley edition/December 1989

ISBN: 0-425-11882-7

A BERKLEY BOOK ® TM 757,375
Berkley Books are published by The Berkley Publishing Group,
200 Madison Avenue, New York, New York 10016.
The name "BERKLEY" and the "B" logo
are trademarks belonging to Berkley Publishing Corporation.

PRINTED IN THE UNITED STATES OF AMERICA.

10 9 8 7 6 5 4 3 2 1

1

Annabelle looked delicious on the dance floor, long-legged, shapely, and flirtatious; she fluttered her dark eyes and swayed her fine hips at him. And Slocum, in a sexual sweat after riding a hard, lonely trail to Bitter Creek, felt the male excitement. He still had the trail through Red River to reach Black Rock, where Tim Blake waited, but surely he had time for this.

They danced, and she brushed her hefty breasts at him, and they talked a bit. Then to his pleasure, she said, "Perhaps we could come to know each other better, Mr. Slocum." Her voice was low and sultry.

"Can't think of anything nicer," he said, impressed by her shameless lust and wondering if his sex appeal got better with time.

She led him to her small house on the edge of town and they quickly stripped, she presenting rosy-tipped breasts and a body with more curves than the trail to Tombstone. Slocum's flesh went ferocious, which made her sigh with pleasure and go at it with vigor. And it didn't take long for him to frolic with her body until the door quietly opened.

The gunman stood there, Colt in hand; he had black eyes in a coarse face, twisted in an evil grin. "Is this polecat tryin' to rape you, Annabelle?" A raucous whiskey voice.

She pulled away from Slocum with a scowl. "That's right, Seth. Forced me. And me a decent, virtuous girl."

Slocum stared at her in shock, his desire dead, aware that, he, too, might suddenly be dead. His clothes and gun were laid on the chair, too far to reach.

"Just a minute, mister," he said.

"Shut up," Seth hissed. He looked at Annabelle. "Move back, I'm goin' to blow him to pieces."

Her eyes widened. "Don't do it, not here, Seth. Don't want a mess."

Seth showed his teeth and stared at Slocum: a big, lean, powerfully muscled hombre with piercing green eyes. Dangerous, Seth thought, and *now* was the best way to tackle him, stripped. But Annabelle didn't want him plastered all over her place, nude and all that. He'd take the polecat outside to the shadows and plug him there.

He reached for Slocum's gun in its holster on the chair and stuck it in his own gunbelt. Then he pushed his thick, coarse face at Slocum. "Teach you to go round rapin' respectable fillies. Get in your duds. And don't make a sound or it's your last."

Slocum silently obeyed, slipping on his blue shirt, then his pants, stumbling as he put one leg in, which brought him close to Seth. Slocum's moves were light-ning fast as his powerful hand shot out, grasping Seth's gun hand, twisting it and forcing the trigger finger. The gun barked as the bullet pierced Seth's chest. He cata-pulted back, shock in his eyes as he realized that death had entered his own body. His black eyes, wide open, fixed on Slocum as he sank down. Then his gaze shifted to Annabelle. Then the light died in his eyes.

Slocum pulled his gun from the dead man's belt and turned to Annabelle. With pale face, hand on breast, she was staring at Seth.

With a quick move of his arm, Slocum slapped her face, leaving the mark of his fingers on her cheek. The sting brought tears to her eyes.

He pulled on his pants and tightened the belt. "You play nasty games, little missy."

She bit her lips. The turnaround had been so sudden, she found it hard to digest.

"Why'd you do it, Annabelle?"

"For money."

He jerked his thumb at the body. "Who is he?"

"Don't know. He gave me twenty dollars to get you here."

Slocum's teeth clenched, and he studied Seth's brutal features. The face was unknown. Just a gunman. Why'd he do it? A grievance? Was he kin to someone Slocum had killed once long ago? No way to know. That hap-pened often—you walked down a street and someone would brace you, swear you shot his kin.

Slocum shrugged. It was a mystery. As for Anna-belle, she was just a paid slut. Did she know anything? He looked at her sternly. "Tell the truth."

"Don't know a damn thing, I swear. He came up to

me at the dance and said, 'There's Slocum, that big, lean hombre over there. I'll give yuh twenty dollars to get him to your place.' 'What are you goin' to do?' I asked him. 'Jest take him with me, that's all.'"

She shook her head. "Didn't dream he was aimin' to shoot you in my place." She looked at him. "After all, Slocum, I did stop him, right?"

Slocum stared at her. She did it more to stop a mess than from concern for his life. He lit a cigarillo and she warily watched him.

"Sorry about it, Slocum." She stood there, naked as a jaybird, with all her curves, still damned sexy, but a bit of a miserable Delilah.

"Mebbe you'd like to finish what we started, Slocum. To tell the truth, I was gettin' some mighty fine lovin'."

His green eyes glinted. "Annabelle, if you were a man, I'd say you had brass balls and you're lucky to be breathin' in and out."

He walked to the door and looked back at Seth, a bloody body. She had a mess plastered all over her room after all.

Outside, he gazed at the big bright stars glittering in the immense Arizona sky, at the great dark bulk of mountains.

Then he started for his horse. His destination was Black Rock. When he thought of that town and what waited for him there, Slocum's teeth clenched hard.

He swung over the powerful roan and started to ride.

Next day, as he rode the trail, Slocum looked at the land, which was rich and glowing under the noonday sun. In the distance, sawtoothed mountains stretched massively to the west. He was on his way to Black Rock but would have to ride through the town of Red River first. He felt hunger pangs and moved the roan to the inviting shade of a nearby cottonwood.

He made a fire, heated beans, ate beef jerky, and, while drinking coffee, he looked at a batch of cotton clouds that hung as if painted in the intense blue sky. Then he pulled Tim Blake's letter from the chest pocket of his blue shirt and read it for the third time.

Dear Slocum,

I need your help. Midge is pregnant. And funny things are happening in Black Rock. Come if you can. Quick.

Tim

Slocum lit a cigarillo, and his green eyes glittered as he thought of Blake. Tim was an old sidekick that he'd known in the war, when Slocum's job had been sharp-shooting the Union brass. On the battlefield, during a sudden charge, Slocum had been cornered by three bluecoats, and Blake had stepped in, shooting fast, getting himself wounded to save Slocum's life. Slocum didn't forget such favors. His jaw clenched; he'd help Blake in Black Rock come hell or high water.

His green eyes were somber as he thought of his past. Of the carpetbagger judge who rode out to claim the Slocum plantation in Georgia. That judge, with Slocum's violent cooperation, found his claim six feet *under* the plantation. It forced Slocum into a life of drifting in the West.

Caught up in memories, Slocum finally noticed the two riders coming slowly down the trail. As they came closer, he studied them coldly. Not the kind he'd trust, from the look of them; he'd seen enough gunslingers in his time. One, a lean, hard-looking man in a yellow vest, said something quietly to the other, then they rode silently until they reached him.

"Howdy," said the man in the vest. "Mosely's the name. We're headed for Bitter Creek."

Slocum stared at the rapine face, deep brown eyes, lean body, and the worn-handled gun in its holster. "You're on the right trail. Stay with it," he said.

"That coffee looks good."

"Real good," said the other man. His narrow face had a stubble beard and light blue eyes. "I'm Clem. Mebbe the gent will be willin' to share?"

Slocum wasn't crazy about the idea of being surrounded by two gunslicks, but they might just take coffee and keep riding. It'd be downright hostile to deny them. "Come ahead."

"Mighty nice of you, mister," said Mosely, swinging gracefully off his Appaloosa, his eyes never leaving Slocum's face, his thin mouth in an ironic twist.

Slocum pulled out a couple of tin cups, and Mosely poured coffee into them.

They sipped from the cups, looking at Slocum almost pleasantly. Then Mosely shook his head. "They jest robbed the bank in Red River. Know that, mister?"

"No."

Clem nodded. "Bold as brass, two riders, shot the teller, cleared out the safe, and hit the trail."

Slocum looked at them and sipped his cup. "Posse go after them?"

"By that time it was too late," said Mosely, his thin mouth in a queer smile.

"How come?" Slocum asked.

"*We* shot the polecats," Mosely said.

"You did? How'd it happen?" Something fishy was going on, but Slocum played it straight.

Mosely's grin was evil. "To tell the truth, we didn't know they were bank robbers. They came up behind us, ridin' hot and heavy, and we thought they were after our hides. So we shot them stone dead."

"Cain't take chances these days," said Clem, also smiling.

Slocum rubbed his chin thoughtfully.

Mosely, with his queer grin, went on. "Reckon you'd say we had a guilty conscience. Like it was the law after us. But when we found five thousand dollars, neatly packed, we realized we had lucked into bank money."

He stopped and waited for Slocum to speak.

Slocum smiled. "Reckon the town was mighty grateful for your efforts."

Mosely looked at Clem and they both laughed. "How in hell you figger that?" He poured another cup of coffee.

Slocum spoke smoothly. "Just jumped to the idea you might have returned the money."

Clem stared hard at Slocum. "That's what you'da done, mister?"

"Reckon so." Slocum kicked at the earth. Strange hombres. Why'd they tell him this, as if it didn't matter one way or another if he knew they were thieves? They were hostile. Why? He thought of Seth, who also had come at him hostile out of nowhere.

Mosely's thin smile was deliberate. "Return the money? We ain't that stupid." His features hardened, as if he expected that Slocum would take offense at the remark.

"You never know right off what stupid is," Slocum said, keeping his hands low. They were seated on the other side of the fire near each other.

"That's not a nice thing to say to the gent, Mosely." Clem's grin belied the words. "Mind if I take another coffee, mister?"

"Help yourself."

"We figgered it smart to keep the money. Do us more good than the bank."

Slocum just shrugged. "You never know what's smart till it's all over."

"But now that you know, mister, you ain't much good to us," said Mosely, frowning, looking closely at Slocum as if for the first time considering he might be more trouble than expected. A man who talked that bold in front of two confessed killers either had to be a fool or dangerous. He turned to Clem, jerking a finger at Slocum. "What d'ya think of this fella?"

"Don't know what to think, Mosely. Talks like a cool head."

"But not too smart, if you think we're two guns against one."

This bothered Clem, who was thinking of something else. "No reason to get agitated, Mosely," he said. "Remember, we're rich men now. Don't do anything reckless."

"What's reckless with this hombre?" demanded Mosely. He stared balefully at Slocum. "You know, mister, you ain't polite. We introduced ourselves. But I noticed you didn't offer your name. Got something to hide, hey?"

"Nothing to hide." Slocum's body was alert. Even before they approached him, he figured them for gunslingers, and within minutes he realized that for some curious reason they wanted a showdown. Yet he didn't know them from Adam. Seemed crazy.

"So, what's your handle, mister?" Mosely's voice was vicious.

"Slocum, John Slocum."

There was a long pause, then Slocum saw something in their eyes. All three rose to their feet, their bodies tense. Slocum could hear the fire crackle, a coyote howl.

"Slocum," said Mosely, "your time has come."

The words were scarcely out of his mouth when Slocum's hand moved, a flash of lightning, his gun barking so fast it sounded like one shot.

Both men had their guns out of their holsters, but only Mosely got off a shot, his bullet hitting the earth. They rocketed back, eyes wide with shock. They lay there dying, red blood pumping from their bodies, spreading over their shirts.

Clem turned painfully to Mosely and whispered, "You stupid bastard. "I tole you we didn't need this. Now we'll never . . . get to . . . spend the money."

Mosely, whose strength was failing fast, muttered, "Only way to go, Clem. Bye." He shut his eyes.

Slocum came up to Clem, who watched with dimming eyes.

"What the hell was all this, Clem? Were you aimin' for me?"

Clem looked at him, his senses failing too fast. He opened his tight lips to speak, but the words sounded like gibberish.

Then his eyes closed.

Slocum pulled the shovel from his saddle pack and dug a grave in the soft earth near a pitted boulder. The sun blistered down, and the skin of his neck prickled with sweat from the heat. He found the neatly packaged bank bills in the saddle pocket of Mosely's Appaloosa. As he looked at the money, he couldn't help think of Clem's last words to Mosely. "You bastard, now we'll never get to spend the money."

Slocum shook his head. That was downright pitiful, wasn't it? For some reason Mosely thought it would be easy to mow him down, and didn't believe the money was at risk. Like all gunslingers, he felt himself invincible. It seemed to be a disease that afflicted many gunmen—the belief in their invincibility. Slocum smiled grimly. But there was always someone out there a fraction of a second faster, and that meant Boot Hill, just as it did for these two polecats.

He dragged their bodies to the open grave and dropped them in.

Feeling impelled to say something, he took off his hat and mumbled, "Mystery to me, God, why you let these ornery critters crawl over your good green earth."

He covered the grave, drank from his canteen, and mopped his brow. Then he swung over the roan and started toward Red River.

The land looked green and fresh, soft rolling hills

under a bright blue sky, with patches of cotton clouds.

Good day to be alive, he thought.

Riding along, Slocum's mind worked on Mosely and Clem. A couple of killers who lucked into bank robbers, who they shot. You'd think they'd be happy with the money and make a getaway or run for the border to spend their ill-gotten gains. But no, they had to stop and, for no sensible reason, engage him in a showdown. Why? Was it because Mosely, in a dumb moment, crowing about shooting the bank robbers, felt they had exposed themselves to Slocum, and for safety, had to wipe him out? Sure had been stupid for him to brag.

Slocum reached a high rise which gave a panoramic view of the land beneath. In the valley, he could see the sun glinting off the roofs of the town sprawled along the twisting stream.

Slocum's mind still worked on the gunslingers. From the moment they rode up to his camp, they seemed hostile. As if nothing would please them more than a showdown. But why? He didn't know them. They even insisted on his name. Odd how they all stood up the moment he spoke it. As if that was the clincher. As if they had to know the name of the man they intended to shoot. Something he saw in Mosely's eyes told him it was showdown time. But why in hell did they want him dead? He never did anything to them.

And what about Seth, back in Bitter Creek. He had used Annabelle for a setup. Was he on target for some reason? Or was it all in his imagination? It was easy to imagine gunfighters were coming out of the walls with one aim, to blast you.

Slocum rubbed his chin. Too much to figure out now. Better put it out of his mind. He'd ride into Red River and return the money to the bank. He touched the money packet in his saddle pack. For a fleeting moment he was tempted, like anyone. What if he kept it? Then he sighed. Belonged mostly to hardworking homesteaders; no, he couldn't do that. He'd return it, get a decent meal, some drinks, and run an eye over the saloon girls before he started for Black Rock.

By noon the next day, as Slocum rode near Red River, the sun looked like a fried egg in a scrubbed blue sky. A light breeze played gently on the cottonwood leaves, which almost made the day tolerable. The coyotes lay quiet in deep shelter from the punishing sun.

There were a few citizens walking on hot Main Street when Slocum reached Red River. He tied the roan to the railing at Berta's Cafe. Six men inside eating looked curiously at the big green-eyed stranger who came in and took a seat near the window.

Berta came up, a smiling, chesty woman, her black eyes gazing at Slocum with interest. "What's your pleasure, mister?"

He looked at her breasts, like that might be a man's pleasure. "Slocum's the name. I'll have chili, beans, biscuits, and coffee."

She grinned. "Where you ridin' in from, Slocum?"

"Bitter Creek."

The men eating surveyed him with interest.

She nodded, "Well, sit easy, I've got the best chili and beans in the territory."

He watched her move toward the kitchen. A muscular cowboy with a red bandanna round his throat spoke up. "Run into any Apaches out there, Slocum?"

He shook his head. "Saw no sign."

"Some renegades prowlin' around."

Slocum nodded, aware that two men at the next table were giving him more than a casual scrutiny.

They turned to each other, picking up their talk, which had stopped when Slocum came through the cafe door. "What I want to know, Healy, is who shot those two damn bank robbers out at Miner's Creek. And where the money went? They didn't have a dime on them. And Bullock is fit to be tied."

"Should be, Amos. He swore they got five thousand dollars. And they shot Preston."

There was a silence. "Figger someone in our bunch, after we spread out, got a shot at them?" Healy asked.

"You figger this someone took off with the money and cached it on the sly?"

"Hate to think that."

There was a silence.

"Of course, it might not be one of our boys. Could be some stranger got them in sight and did the shootin'."

They turned to look at Slocum. Then Healy said, "But how'd he know they hit the bank?"

Berta brought out his chili and put it down with a smile. "Try that, mister."

Slocum tasted it and found it delicious. "Real good."

She looked pleased. "Stayin' in town, Slocum?"

"Ridin' to Black Rock."

"Sorry to hear that. You might like Red River."

A new customer came in, and Berta went over to him.

Then Amos said, "Ask him, Healy, go ahead, ask him."

"Say, Slocum. Did you happen to run into a couple

of robbers? They did some killin' here and ran off with the bank money."

Slocum put a forkful of chili into his mouth and chewed thoughtfully. "Didn't run into robbers. But ran into a coupla gunslingers who had a packet of money."

Everyone stopped eating and stared at Slocum.

"I'll be damned," said Amos. "How'd you know they had this money?"

"They told me," Slocum said, calmly eating.

"Told you how they got it?"

Slocum nodded. "Shot a coupla bank robbers, they said."

There was a long silence.

"Why in hell did they tell you that, mister?" said Healy.

"Damned if I know. I think they didn't care, since they expected to leave me croaked."

Nobody was eating. "But you ain't croaked," said a short, stocky cowboy at the corner table.

"Glad you noticed," said Slocum cheerfully.

Again a silence.

"Mebbe *they're* croaked, Mullins," said Amos to the short cowboy.

Slocum mopped up the chili on his plate and nodded. "You got it, Amos. They're croaked and I'm not."

You could have heard a pin drop.

Nobody spoke until Healy, his blue eyes gleaming, said slowly, "Then you must have the money."

"I got it. In my saddlebag."

There was a big let-out of air, as if the men had been holding their breath.

"I reckon you might be bringing that money back to Red River or you'd never come this way," Amos said.

"Sounds like mighty good reasoning," said Slocum. He wiped his mouth, stood up, and paid Berta. The men followed him out to the roan.

He pulled the money out of his saddlebag.

They stared at it. Healy said, "Well, Slocum, you're one cool customer. We figgered that money lost. And Bullock is goin' to be mighty pleased 'bout this."

The Red River Bank was a solid oak building with a dull yellow window. Looking through it, Slocum could see a gray-haired man with a square face talking to a young man in a white shirt. Slocum, with Healy and Amos as escort, walked through the heavy doors.

Healy grinned from ear to ear. "Mr. Bullock, I want you to meet this gent, by the name of Slocum. He's got something for you."

Bullock looked up. A heavy-boned face with small penetrating eyes. His face had a scowl that seemed never to have left it since the robbery. "Something for me? Like what?"

"Like bank money," said Healy.

Bullock looked startled, then stared at Healy. "*My* bank money. He's got it?"

"Yeah, I got it," said Slocum.

"Where? Where is it?" He glared at Slocum as if it was outrageous that he should be separated from his money one second longer than necessary.

With a small smile at Bullock's agitation, Slocum opened his bag and pulled out the neatly wrapped bills.

Bullock's eyes went saucer wide and his thick hands darted to the bundle, like a mother to her infant. "The money!" he gasped. He examined the binding, still untouched, and, aware that not even one precious dollar had been molested, his face twisted in a joyous grin.

"God, it's the money." He stared at Slocum in wonder, trying to figure out how the money had come to him. His eyes ran a gamut of feelings: wonder, curiosity, suspicion. He looked at Healy then at Slocum.

"Slocum is it? How the hell did you get this money?"

Slocum pulled a cigarillo from his pocket and lit up.

Healy spoke quickly. "He shot two gunslingers, Bullock. Shot 'em and took the money."

Healy looked admiringly at the big, lean man. "Slocum, you gotta be fast as Billy the Kid to knock off those two gunslingers."

Bullock looked sharply at Slocum, as if he found the situation unbelievable. He studied Slocum. "You shot the two rotten dogs who killed Preston?"

Slocum felt weary. "It's a long story, and I don't want to get into it. Couple of low-down gunslingers on the trail got mean, and for some reason wanted my hide. I had to protect myself, so I shot 'em. They had your money."

"How in hell did *they* get it?"

"They told me they shot the robbers and took it, that's how."

"And you shot them? Two of them? How?"

A small smile twisted Slocum's lips. "A straight shootout."

"You faced them down? Shot against two guns?" Bullock's voice was strained with disbelief.

Slocum bit his lips. He was getting very tired. "Mr. Bullock, you got your money, that's the main thing." He turned to go.

"Just a minute, Slocum." Bullock's eyes gleamed.

"Sounds like you did somethin' special. This town is mighty grateful. I'd like to offer you a reward."

Slocum shook his head. "Did what any right-minded man would do." He turned quickly and walked out the door.

Bullock scowled, staring after him.

Slocum walked toward the saloon, his boots clumping on the wooden boardwalk.

The low sun streaked the sky with yellow and orange and singed the mountains with fire.

2

It was a big saloon with plenty of customers at the bar
and the poker tables. There was a space at the bar near a
lean, narrow-faced cowboy in a black shirt. He was
wearing two tied-down guns and looked dangerous and
mean, a gunfighter. It was easy to see why nobody
wanted to crowd him. He'd been drinking whiskey for
some time, but he showed no signs of it except for the
mean look.

When Slocum stepped to the space beside the gunman, the man didn't move to make it easier for Slocum.
His cold black eyes skidded over Slocum as if he was
some strange bug, then his gaze went back to the redhead seated at a table with a young cowboy. She was
pretty, with hazel eyes and light skin, and she wore a
silky green dress with deep cleavage.

For a moment Slocum was irritated at the surly gunfighter and thought of straightening him out. The man looked vicious—the kind of hombre who if pushed would go for his gun. Slocum, thinking of Seth, Clem, and Mosely, figured he had had enough gunplay for a time. What he wanted was relaxation.

The barman, who was bald and round-faced, with careful eyes, came up and smiled. He seemed impressed that Slocum dared to crowd the gunman. "What's your pleasure, mister?"

"Whiskey."

The barman poured a glass and left the bottle. Slocum gulped one drink and poured another.

The swinging doors opened and Healy and Amos pushed through, grinned at him, and settled in a nearby space as two men left the bar.

Slocum brought the glass to his lips and watched the girl in the green dress. She looked slightly bored by the young cowboy, who was flushed from drinking. If she was aware of the gunman's steady stare, she didn't show it. But Slocum's gaze grabbed her, and she wreathed her lips in a smile and stretched her round arms, which made her lovely breasts strain against the silky dress. Showing the merchandise, Slocum thought, amused.

And looking at her curves, he thought she had plenty of them. The gunfighter also seemed to think so, for he grunted and walked to her table.

"Howdy," he said to her, ignoring the cowboy.

She looked at him without feeling, blinking her eyes. The cowboy glanced up with a slight frown.

"You're a real honeybunch," the gunfighter said. "I'm Kirk."

"That's nice to know," she said without enthusiasm.

She jerked her thumb at the cowboy. "He's Tom. Been drinking a bit."

The cowboy's face was sullen. "I can handle it, Daisy."

"Didn't say you couldn't." Her voice was apologetic.

The gunfighter's mean face stared at the cowboy. "This here cowboy looks real tired. Needs to go some-where for a lie-down."

The cowboy had enough drink in him to make him dull to danger, for he bristled. "Lie-down? I don't need a lie-down."

The gunfighter's black eyes grew smaller. "Yeah, you do, kid. Mebbe you oughta find yourself a cradle somewhere and sleep it off. You been tying up this here honeybunch long enough."

Again the cowboy bristled, though he didn't open his eyes wide enough to see who had accosted him. "Who the hell do you think you are? You come over, rude as hell, interrupting me when I'm sitting here with this filly. Who the hell are you?"

Slocum could see the cowboy's mind was clouded with booze, and he had small awareness of who he was tangling with.

The gunfighter's black eyes were cold as death. "Who am I? I'm the man who's goin' to put a bullet in your head if you don't stand up and walk out that door."

A deep hush went over the saloon as the customers smelled the presence of sudden death.

The meaning of the words struck the cowboy like a whip, his face paled, and he suddenly sobered. He stared at the gunfighter, seeing him clearly for the first time, lean and hard, built for speed. He saw the danger to himself.

"Maybe you better go, Tom," Daisy said softly. "We don't want trouble."

The cowboy, glad of an out, seemed ready, Slocum thought, to go out and live. But he made the mistake of looking at the gunfighter, whose face was grinning with contempt. The gunfighter's gaze then shifted to Daisy, and lechery gleamed in his black eyes.

The cowboy was suddenly flooded with rage. He came to his feet. "Draw, you dog," he hissed.

The words were scarcely out of his mouth when the sound of a pistol barked and the cowboy stood petrified, a bullet hole in his forehead. He quivered like a tree hit by lightning and fell back.

The gunfighter's face was pitiless as he turned to look at the watching crowd. "I warned him," he said softly and slipped his gun back into its holster.

The barman signaled two men who picked up the dead cowboy, lugging him through the swinging doors. The sounds and revelry of the saloon started again, and there seemed no way to know there'd been a showdown.

The gunfighter had gone back to the bar, feeling it too soon to press his attentions on Daisy. The seat beside her stayed empty, probably the result of the gunfighter's interest in her. He made that interest mighty clear, for he leaned against the bar, his elbows on it, and stared at her. Only once did he glance at Slocum, his black eyes cold and expressionless.

Daisy looked gloomy, wondering if somehow she'd been the cause of the cowboy's death.

The barman brought her a bottle and a glass and spoke in a low voice as he poured. She shrugged her shoulders and nursed the drink. Finally her gaze strayed to Slocum, and, pleased at what she saw, she smiled.

To her astonishment, and that of others in the saloon, Slocum drifted to her table and sat down. "You all right?" he asked.

She was startled, and her eyes darted to the frowning gunfighter. "Maybe," she said.

"Not busy?" he asked.

She couldn't help smile at his nerve. "Not right now."

"You might not be in the mood for pleasuring," he said.

Her hazel eyes went over him and glowed with interest. "You look like you could put a woman in the mood for pleasuring."

"Then why don't we try," he said, figuring it might be smart to act fast to forestall the jealous polecat at the bar.

"Come after me," she said, and when she stood suddenly, he followed her quickly up the stairs.

It all happened so fast the gunfighter watching them was bewildered for a second. Then he realized that Slocum had outfoxed him. His face settled in a fury. He turned to the bar, brought the whiskey bottle to his mouth, and chugged it.

Slocum shut the door behind him and closed it with its key.

The room had a big bed, a single chair, and a red painted bureau with a washbasin and a water pitcher on it.

"What's your name?"

"Slocum."

"Slocum, you've got nerve. It made me sick, the

way that polecat gunned down poor Tom."

Slocum nodded. "He's jealous. That's why he did it."

She nodded slowly, looking at him with slight amazement. "Hope you know what you're doin'. But you sure got nerve." She drew back to study him. "And you look like you can handle yourself."

He gazed at her hips, her breasts. "Rather handle you," he said.

"What are we waitin' for?" She unbuttoned her dress and let it fall. She had shapley breasts, a flat stomach, and a nice round curve of hips.

He pulled off his clothes, and his erect flesh captured her attention. "That's a proper-looking member." She took charge and did some extraordinary things.

Afterward his hands caressed her breasts and buttocks. She pressed against him and brought him to the bed. His hands explored her body, her rounded buttocks, her thighs, and, between them, her moist triangle. They came together, and, as she felt him, she sighed with pleasure. They moved slowly, building to a powerful rhythm, and Slocum, his mood fiery, started to drive. Her body pumped fiercely against his, and she unleashed groans until they both hit climax. She held her breath, her body twisting as if in agony.

They went still. Finally, in a faint voice, she said, "That was fine lovin', Slocum."

After they dressed Daisy spoke slowly. "You might wait while I go and see if things have simmered down."

Slocum adjusted his gunbelt with a smile. "What the hell does that mean, honeybunch?"

Her gaze was sharp. "That's what I mean. That ugly

customer downstairs who called me 'honeybunch' is goin' to kick up some fierce dust."

"Reckon he might." Slocum's voice was cool.

"I'll try and settle his feathers." She started for the door.

"Don't do that," he said.

She turned. "He's a terrible, mean mongrel. A dangerous gunfighter. I got the cowboy's blood on my conscience. Don't want your blood, too." She sighed. "Especially yours, Slocum. You'd be a terrible loss to the ladies."

He laughed. "That so? I'm mighty grateful, honey. But the time hasn't come for me to hide behind a lady's skirts."

Her gaze was direct. "I could distract him."

He smiled. "Like a cow does a red-eyed bull? No. I'll just go down alongside you and wait for the bull to throw his horns."

She fixed her dress and walked to the door. "You might let me try to get his attention."

He shook his head. "You won't be able to do anything. He's goin' to pull that gun, no matter what. He don't look a forgiving type of man."

"No, he doesn't." She opened the door, walked down the hall, turned, and started down the steps.

Slocum paused to light a cigarillo, then followed her.

The talk and clink of glasses seemed to go quiet as the crowd in the bar sighted Slocum.

Earlier, when Slocum had waltzed off with the filly, he had left the gunfighter in a steaming rage. The liquored crowd had read it and loved it. They had been stunned by the cool style of the green-eyed stranger. Somehow he had seemed to mock the jealous gunfighter, whose blazing speed had mowed down the cowboy.

Sullenly, the gunfighter continued to drink at the bar, then had gone to a poker table, taking a seat facing the stairs. As Daisy came down the stairs, much as she detested the gunfighter, she tried to engage his black eyes. Their cold fury sent a tremor of fear through her. Then he looked at Slocum coming after her, and his mean mouth tightened in a wolfish smile.

"Hey."

Slocum in ironic amusement gazed side to side, as if the gunman might be talking to someone else. Then he pointed to himself, questioning.

It was a comic pantomime, and the spectators grinned at each other, aware they were on the verge of seeing some entertaining fireworks.

"You look like a man who likes gambling," said the gunfighter.

Slocum sauntered toward the table. "Yeah, I like it."

"You could join us, mebbe win a little money." His smile broadened.

There were four seated players at the table.

"Like to," said Slocum. "But your table looks full up."

The gunfighter showed yellow teeth. "We'll make room." He turned to stare at a pale-skinned cowhand sitting opposite him.

The cowhand coughed gently and stood. "I've had enough." His voice was cracked. "Take my seat, mister."

The gunfighter grinned. "Polite folks in this town. Makes ya feel at home. Sit down. Deal him in, Jimmy," he said to a rangy, curly-haired cowboy.

Jimmy nodded, staring at Slocum with the curiosity with which you'd look at a dead man. "Sure, sure, Kirk," he said.

"That's my handle," Kirk said, watching Jimmy shuffle, then waiting for Slocum to present his name.

But Slocum just glanced at the corner of the saloon where Daisy had positioned herself, as if the last thing she wanted was to witness a slaughter.

The gunfighter picked up Slocum's glance. "Yeah," he said. "Folks here are mighty friendly."

"Friendly enough," Slocum said.

"Specially the ladies." Kirk's voice was sarcastic.

Slocum smiled, stared into the black eyes, then picked up his cards.

An icy glaze came to the gunfighter's eyes. He couldn't help think of what had gone on in the room upstairs. A shiver of anger went through his hard body.

The first draw was won by Jimmy with a pair of tens. The gunfighter gathered the cards and shuffled. Slocum studied him; he seemed to be in no hurry for a showdown. He was playing a game. A professional killer, he liked some amusement before he pulled his gun. This feeling of play in the gunfighter had been fired with particular force in the case of Slocum.

"You look like a man who's been around," Kirk said to Slocum. "Why don't you tell us something about yourself?"

"Why?"

The gunfighter's grin broadened. "It's friendly, mister. We're interested. We wanna know somethin' 'bout you. Ain't that right, Jimmy?"

"If you say so, Kirk."

"What d'ya want to know?" Slocum asked.

"Where're you from?"

"Calhoun County, Georgia."

"Well, I knew you were a rebel. You rebels didn't do too good in the war. But that's over. Funny thing, we don't know your name. Don't know what to call you."

"Slocum's the name."

Something went off in the gunfighter's brain. Slocum saw it. It was recognition. He became less playful, even a bit cautious.

"So you're Slocum," he said finally.

"Yeah, that's me."

The gunfighter nodded. "Heard about you."

"You did? And what was what?"

The gunfighter hitched his shoulders. "That you ain't the slowest gun in the territory."

"Where'd you hear that?"

Kirk paid no attention to the question. He seemed to be thinking. Then he said, "Didn't expect you to get *this* far, Slocum. You're better than some folks think."

Slocum scowled. "What do you mean, 'this far'?"

"To here, this place."

Slocum scowled. Suddenly he thought of Seth, of Clem and Mosely. They had all pulled their guns. Why? To stop him? And this gunfighter seemed to know about it. Slocum took a deep breath. So he'd been on target after all. Somebody was trying to stop him.

Then Kirk grinned. "Well, you won't get to Black Rock. That's the main thing."

Slocum's eyes narrowed. "What the hell do you mean?"

The gunfighter ignored the question. "Shoulda figured you to be Slocum, when you grabbed the filly. That took nerve." His black eyes glowed.

Slocum's jaw was hard. "You ain't the first who tried to stop me from getting to Black Rock. Why?"

The gunfighter seemed to harden, coiling like a rattler before striking. He spoke slowly. "Yours is not to ask why. Just to draw and die." As he came to his feet, Slocum did too.

The gunfighter then drawled, "I hate to do this. Just pulled a pair of aces."

As the last word left his lips, his hand moved with dazzling speed and his gun came up, but it was the second of two shots that blasted the silence of the saloon.

The bullet hit his face like a gigantic fist and he was flung back. He went down slowly, his features twisted in shock. His eyes stayed on Slocum in wonder as he died.

Slocum came out of the saloon under a glowing half-moon that silvered the tops of the humpbacked mountains in the distance. He sauntered down the main street, passing the livery, the cafe, and the general store. Yellow lamplight filtered through the house windows and spread on the street.

Slocum's mood was somber as he moved toward the hotel. He thought of the gunfighter, Kirk, who had said, 'Never expected you to reach here.'

That was one hell of a remark. What could it mean? Did Kirk know about the gunmen who had tried to shoot him down?

Like Seth, who had hired Annabelle to set him up for target practice? Like Clem and Mosely? They had bragged about grabbing the bank money, and could have decided, after that, it was too dangerous to let him live. Was that the reason? Or did they have him as a target and didn't care what he knew? What Kirk knew was gone forever now.

It was all a riddle.

Tim Blake's letter was an appeal for him to come. But some gunmen wanted to stop Slocum dead in his tracks.

He walked into the OK Hotel, where the clerk was dozing in the corner. He scuffed his boots and the clerk's eyes opened. He came up smiling, a small balding man with wide ears.

"Yes sir, what can I do for you?"

"Room for the night."

"Yessir, got a nice one to the front."

It was a good room with a big, soft bed that promised comfort.

Slocum appreciated the softness of a mattress after countless nights of sleeping on the trail.

He walked out on the porch. A soft south wind brought the scent of tangy grass. By this time the moon had climbed high and cast silver and deep mysterious shadows on the mountains. Slocum, who had a taste for the beauties of nature, couldn't help but think of how endless was the time of the mountains and how short the span of a man's life—especially those who lived by the gun. The threat of sudden death was ever present in the wild western territories. And as Slocum thought of Black Rock he seemed to hear, sharper than ever, the sound of gunfire.

He sighed and went back to the room and stretched out on the bed.

3

Tim Blake rode to the hilltop, wheeled his pinto, and looked back down at his ranch. He had the habit of doing this before he rode the trail into Black Rock. It gave him pleasure to look at this piece of land that he had built with the sweat of his brow. A nice hunk of earth, with cattle, horses, a solid ranch house, and best of all, a fine stream.

He felt sure that the big rancher, John Grant, his wealthy neighbor, had secretly craved this stream. Once Grant had made an offer on it. Tim didn't want to sell, but he offered to let Grant use it. Grant turned him down. Funny thing about Grant. He didn't like to owe anything to anyone. Grant was a proud, rich man.

Tim thought some more about Grant, and his face began to darken. He didn't like his thoughts, and when his wife, Midge, came out of the house he was glad he could think instead, about her. Even from that hilltop, he could see her rounded belly, and his intense blue eyes glowed as he thought about it. His childhood sweetheart, a beautiful, willful girl whom he had loved since she wore pigtails back in Georgia. He had married her after he'd come out of the fighting, still cursed with a rotten war wound.

Then his thoughts shifted suddenly to his troubles, which had been coming hard at him lately in Black Rock. The gunfighters. His craggy face tightened. Tim Blake was lean, sinewy, with short curly hair and keen blue eyes that had looked on his fellows without fear. Yet these last months he had been besieged. He felt closed in and needed help. That's when he wrote Slocum, his sidekick in the war. He'd been fiercely loyal to Slocum, whom he admired. His war wound, which still dogged him, he had got while defending Slocum from a sneak attack. So he wrote Slocum, asking him to come fast to Black Rock. He wondered if it was already too late. His heart was heavy as he looked again at his ranch, and at Midge walking back toward the house.

He wheeled the pinto west and started to ride.

He'd ride the trail into Black Rock and try to keep out of trouble, at least till Slocum came.

Once Slocum gets here, things will be safe, he told himself.

He put the pinto into a faster gait.

His destination was the Deadeye Saloon.

Rightly named.

From the ridge Slocum could see a craggy slope climbing steeply from a gully. Directly in front lay the Blake ranch, a gently undulating green spread in the late sun.

Rich grass and grazing cattle. A stream meandered through the land, which made it special. Water, the most precious element, nourished the land, the animals, and the human creatures living on it.

There was a sturdy frame house, with its white paint peeling, and there were three horses in the corral.

Slocum nudged the roan down toward the house, a bit mystified by the quiet.

Before he reached the ranch, a short, rotund Mexican woman came out of the house with washing, which she began to hang on a nearby line. Glancing about, she saw Slocum, which seemed to alarm her, for she went barreling back into the house.

Moments later a woman in a loose gingham dress came out, and he recognized Midge. Her blond hair glowed in the sinking sun, but her body showed the soft rounding of pregnancy. She shielded her eyes to stare at him, then did a small dance of joy, as if nothing could be more pleasing to her eyes. Riding closer, Slocum looked far off, where the cattle grazed, and noted two small figures. Would one be Tim?

As he nudged the roan to a faster pace toward the ranch house, he felt the wind of a bullet as it sang past his ear and heard the sound bounce off the crags. Instinctively he ducked close to the horse, jerking his rifle from the saddle holster, his eyes scanning the land behind him. High on the slope, in a tortuous, pileup of flinty crags, he caught the gleam of sun on metal. Slocum sighted and fired.

The small figure of a man suddenly appeared, staggering, grabbing at his throat. He tottered, then fell forward, his body tumbling over and over the rocks, hitting them like a rag doll until he dropped into the depths of the ravine.

Slocum got down off the horse and waited, kneeling with his rifle ready, but nothing moved on the crags. Convinced the bushwhacker had been alone, Slocum slipped cautiously onto the roan and continued to ride to the ranch.

When he reached Midge, he swung off the horse, glancing back. "Someone tried to bushwhack me," he said.

She scowled and stared at the faraway cliff. "Oh God, these guns, these terrible guns."

Slocum gazed at her slightly rounded belly. She had reason to be upset. She was creating life, while all around in the territory they were trying to kill it.

He looked at Midge and smiled. Most men looking at Midge would smile; she was lovely, with golden silk hair, a delicate turned-up nose, violet eyes in an oval face, and with skin that seemed luminous from her pregnancy.

Expecting a smile in turn, he was jarred by the curious pain in her eyes, since her little dance expressed a different feeling.

"John, John," she murmured, "it's so good to see you."

She held him tightly, then drew away, and he was startled at the tears brimming in her eyes.

"What is it?" he asked.

Her lips pressed tightly together, as if nothing would force her to speak. She looked unseeing into the distance, then spoke in a cracked voice. "It's Tim. He's dead."

The words hit Slocum hard, he couldn't digest it. "Dead?" he repeated mechanically.

She nodded. And her tears flowed. She clasped him to her again, as if his touch would magically restore her dead husband.

Slocum patted her shoulders, his face hard. He thought of the letter. "Trouble in Black Rock." He thought of Tim, his square, honest face, his ready rough humor as they slogged through the drudgery of the war. He thought of the moment Tim had stepped between him and death.

"Let's go in the house," Midge said.

Slocum's heart went out to her, alone now, with Tim's baby on the way.

The ranch house was simple, with plain wooden furnishings. They sat at the table, while Rosa, the Mexican maid, brought out coffee and whiskey. Slocum was feeling rotten and poured himself a hefty drink.

Midge sat opposite him, sipping coffee. Slocum watched, not wanting to push her to talk until she was ready.

Her troubled violet eyes gazed at him. "It happened in town at the Deadeye Saloon. Some hard words between Tim and this gunfighter. Tim didn't want to fight, because of me and the baby. But things got bad between them, an argument. Tim lost his temper." She took a deep breath. "They brought him here, all shot up."

Slocum's face was hard, remembering Tim as a quick gun in the old days. But he thought Tim had settled down. Well, did a man like Tim Blake ever settle down? He always had an exploding point.

Tim Blake had saved his life in the war, got himself wounded. Slocum owed him one.

"Who was he, the gunfighter?"

"I don't know. Someone called him Slade. Poor Tim was dead. I didn't think beyond that. Buried him behind the house." She shook her head. "I won't get over this."

"Sorry I didn't get here sooner," Slocum said.

"Things were getting ugly."

Slocum thought of the letter Tim had sent. He'd write like that only if things got hot. He always kept trouble to himself. And Slocum remembered he had plenty after his wound. He brought Tim's letter from his chest pocket and read it aloud. "Funny things are happening in Black Rock."

Her violet eyes looked puzzled.

"What things?" he asked.

She stared at him. "Let me see that?" She scanned it. "Oh, yes, I remember. It was the fighting. He kept getting into fights. He said he'd been forced to pull his gun. I was worried sick. I pleaded with him not to go to the Deadeye Saloon. But you know Tim. He wasn't going to be bulldozed into staying away."

She sighed. "Oh, Slocum. I'm so unhappy." Her lovely face was twisted with anguish.

His jaw tightened. He had already determined to confront the gunfighter, Slade, who had struck down Blake. "Is there anything I can do, Midge?"

"If you'd have been here, it might have helped. He always listened to you."

Slocum looked thoughtful. You can't tell a man not to avenge an insult. He had to make up his own mind whether to pull his gun or not. There was a code in the territory. He looked at Midge, such a pretty thing. And pregnant. What would happen to her now?

"Those fights at the Deadeye," he said. "When Tim

said 'funny things happening' did he mean the shootouts at the saloon? Was that it?"

Midge frowned. "I don't know. There was drinking and fighting."

He finished off his whiskey. Then through the window he saw a rider on a beautiful Morgan, followed by three cowboys. They were headed for the house.

"You've got visitors," Slocum said.

She glanced through the window. "That's John Grant, our neighbor, a fine man. Very helpful. He sent a couple of his men after the gunfighter, to pay him off for what he did to Tim."

Slocum turned to look at the man who had dismounted and was coming toward the house. Fine-looking, broad-shouldered, powerful, with a rough-hewn handsome face. He came through the door, his expression serious.

After Midge introduced them, she said, "Slocum knew Tim in the war, Mr. Grant. They were sidekicks."

The gray eyes in Grant's strong, rugged face stared at Slocum. "Glad to meet you. Blake was a square shooter. Proud to have him as a friend." He sat down at the table, poured a whiskey, and gulped it down.

"I've got the ranch just upland. I admired Tim Blake. He mentioned you. Told about the close calls he had in the war. He was wounded."

Slocum lifted his whiskey glass. "He got that wound stepping between me and a couple of bluecoats. They were out to finish me off."

Grant's gray eyes shone with interest. "Did he? I knew him as a man of guts. Can't tell you how sorry I was that Slade mowed him down."

Slocum's jaw hardened. "Who is this damned Slade?"

"Gunfighter. Whenever he gets drunk, he wants to kill. A quarrelsome dog." Grant looked at his whiskey glass. "I sent Mason and Lucas, two of my best gunmen, after him. We don't need coyotes like that ruinin' the territory."

Slocum nodded. Grant seemed a decent man. He'd hang around Black Rock until Grant's men came back. If they came back. Till then he'd do what he could for Midge.

Grant toyed with his glass. "You at loose ends right now, Slocum? If so, you could join us."

"Like what?"

"I can always use a good man. I've got a thousand head, and there's rustlers about. Don't know what your experience is, but I figure most men are no damn good. Give 'em a chance to steal, they'll do it."

Slocum rubbed his jaw. "There's plenty like that, Mr. Grant. But there's good folks, too."

Grant looked thoughtful. "There's been wild gunmen driftin' through town lately, been fightin' and shootin'. A low element. This town's gettin' like Tombstone."

"One of them shot at me as I rode in here," Slocum said.

Grant's face hardened. "Seem to be shootin' at anyone, for target practice. Gotta clean out these scum."

Midge had been listening to them as she sipped her coffee. "There's plenty of coyotes walking around looking like men," she said. "Like the one who shot my husband, the father of my child." The thought of her unborn child touched her feelings, and her voice cracked. "Sometimes it's hard to keep going."

A look of pity came over Grant's rough face. "Midge, I'd like to make an offer, and I hope it won't be misunderstood. I'd like you to call on me for help. Money to pay your boys. To sell your cattle. Any help I can give you." He lifted his glass. "We've been good neighbors. And I've got more money than I know what to do with."

Midge's eyes were brimming with tears. "Mr. Grant, I consider myself fortunate to have you for a friend."

She turned. "You, too, Slocum."

Grant walked to the door. "Midge, I know you're too proud to come to my ranch and ask for help. So from time to time I'm goin' to drop by and see what's needed."

He looked sadly at her, nodded to Slocum, and went out the door, where his escort, three wide-shouldered cowboys, had been leaning on the corral fence smoking and talking.

Grant swung over his saddle, tipped his hat toward the house, and, followed by his men, started to ride off.

"Mighty fine man," Slocum said.

"A real friend." They walked out under the darkening sky. A pale moon in the east was climbing from behind the mountain peaks. The light breeze carried the scent of grasses.

"So what do you aim to do, Slocum?"

"I don't know yet. Mosey into town and find out what happened to Slade. I'll stick around in case Grant's guns run into trouble."

Slocum's face hardened as he thought of Tim trying to avoid a showdown because of his family, but being forced into it by Slade, a vicious drunk.

"It's getting late, you could stay the night."

He looked at her. She seemed so delicate, yet he sensed a lot of strength in her. She was carrying a child, and determined to survive. That was nature.

His eyes idly wandered up to the craggy incline, and he thought of the unprovoked shooting. "Have you lost any of your men, Midge?"

"That's curious. We have. Two. Sam and Tad Jones, brothers who worked for us. Why'd you ask?"

"How'd you lose them?"

"Fights. In town. The usual thing. Someone drinking too much, going off the handle. Pulling guns." She stared at him again. "Why'd you ask?"

"I don't know. Seems like a lot of bullets are flying around here. Wonder if there's some purpose behind it. Or if it's just wild bullets."

"Purpose? What purpose?"

He shrugged. "I wouldn't begin to know that, Midge. But don't bother your head about it. There's just one thing on my mind right now, and that's Slade."

She leaned against the corral fence. "A bad man, and a dangerous gunfighter, this Slade. It's too late for Tim. Even if you shoot Slade, it won't bring Tim back. And we might lose you. Might be better to forget that rotten coyote."

Slocum smiled coldly. "No. Slade shot Tim. He's got to pay."

She shrugged. "So be it. You were always a true friend to Tim. I knew you'd stick with him to the end."

"To the end."

Before she went into the house, she kissed him lightly on the cheek. "Thank you for being here, Slocum."

•   •   •

The moon was climbing higher, silvering the mountain peaks. Slocum, sitting on the corral fence, had been watching a fine sorrel pace the ground restlessly. Then he saw the two cowhands riding in from the range, one tall and lean, the other short and muscular, wearing a black flat hat. They dismounted near him.

The lean man strolled over and lit up a cigar. "Howdy. I'm Ed."

"Slocum."

"So you're Slocum." His dark eyes looked at him straight. "Tim Blake thought a helluva lot of you." He jerked his thumb at the other cowboy. "That's Bill."

Slocum nodded to Bill. "Too bad about Tim," he said. "Did you men see the showdown?"

"Yeah, I saw it," said Ed.

"What happened?" Slocum leaned forward.

Ed shook his head, and a sour look came over him as he remembered. He came closer to Slocum and looked thoughtful. "This Slade's a mean gunfighter. Came in from Tombstone. Oh, he's soft and easy till he drinks. Then he changes. Turns mean as a rattler. Just as soon shoot you as look at you. He's standing next to Tim. Suddenly he says, 'Hey, you're crowdin' me, mister.' He's starin' at Tim.

"Tim didn't like it, but he wasn't eager for quarrelin'. He'd been warned by Midge not to get into drinkin' fights. So he says 'You can have room if you want it.' He steps back.

"Slade looks disgruntled that he wasn't goin' to get a fight. So he twists his mouth ugly and says, 'You goddamn rebels are always pushin.' But you can't fight. Or won't. No wonder you damned coyotes lost the war.'

"That hit Tim where it hurt. He turned toward him,

his face pale. 'Them's fightin' words, if I ever heard any. But I know you been drinkin' and your brains are muddled. So you're just jabberin'. And I'm in a gentle mood. So let's let it go by. Right, mister?'

"Slade's got black eyes, and they looked like they were goin' to burn right through his head.

"'Wrong, mister. You call it gentle, but I call it yellow. A streak big and yellow goin' all the way down your back.' And his ugly face grins.

"Well, that did it. Poor Tim. The taste for killin' Slade was in him so bad, he couldn't stop.

"He said, 'Hey, Slade. You remind me of some slimy thing crawlin' out of a hole. Why don't you crawl back in, so nobody can hear you?'

"There was this dead silence, then Slade said 'Goddam rebel, reckon you got some guts after all. But I'm goin' to have to kill you.' Everyone ran for the walls.

"They faced each other, and Slade's gun hand moved like a streak."

Ed shook his head sorrowfully. "Poor Tim, he went down, and I saw it in his eyes. His grief. Losing the draw, losing his woman, losing his life."

Slocum's green eyes gleamed venomously. Tim had been forced into a fight by a vicious, quarrelsome gunslick. A fast gunfighter. Why'd he pick on Tim? Was it just because he'd been drinking and turned into a killing dog? Was he just fighting the polecat who happened to be crowding him? Or did he have a clear idea who he was fighting?

What the hell was going on in Black Rock? Sam and Tad Jones, shot. He himself had been a target of gunfighters ever since Bitter Creek. Were these wild guns, or was something else going on?

Slocum wanted some answers. Would Slade have an answer? If he did, it would pay to track him down. No point staying here. It was a waste of time. Best to get on the trail of this Slade mongrel and try to shake the truth out of him.

He smiled at the two men. "You boys are worried about payday, I reckon, now that Tim's gone."

Bill nodded. "Yeah, it's worrisome."

Slocum hitched his belt. "Mr. Grant aims to stand behind Midge. You'll get your wages."

Ed and Bill looked at each other. "That's nice to know. He's a real gentleman, John Grant is."

Slocum walked toward the ranch house. He'd tell Midge that he was going into town. Grant's two gunfighters were on Slade's trail, but Slade was a real hardcase.

Slocum's jaw clenched. He had to find out what was happening.

4

The moon lay a carpet of silver over the dust of the main street in Black Rock as Slocum walked the roan toward the Deadeye Saloon. There were a few miners on the street, bearded, rugged, and ready for fun. They'd been working all week and now wanted cards, women, and fights—not necessarily in that order.

Some men staggered down the street, swilling from bottles. They seemed in good spirits, not hostile, and waved good-humoredly at Slocum, liking the sight of the lean, rugged-looking cowboy riding a spirited horse. He stopped in front of the Deadeye Saloon, from which flowed voices raised in song and laughter.

He tied the roan to the railing and had just stepped onto the porch in front of the batwing doors when they were suddenly flung open and a young cowboy came hurtling out, back first. There was no way Slocum could

evade the stumbling body, which struck him at an awk-
ward angle, and both the cowboy and he went down on
the boardwalk in a flurry of arms and legs.

A massive, muscled man, whose fists seemed to be
the source of the cowboy's explosive exit, came through
the door, followed by several men. The unexpected
sight of the two men with arms and legs entangled on
the ground seemed to them hugely comic, for they burst
into jeering laughter.

Slocum, without a shred of dignity, looked up from
the ground, at the red, flushed, grinning faces.

"Hey, stranger," said the massive cowboy to him.
"You sure picked a bad moment to come into the Deadeye." That sent the watching men into another gale of
laughter.

"You hit one but got two, Mullins," said one on-
looker.

Mullins, the hugely muscled man, glared at the
young cowboy lying almost flat out, blood leaking from
the sides of his mouth. "You've got a big mouth, Jocko.
Now it's bloody. You're mighty lucky I pulled my
punch."

By this time, Slocum had untangled himself from the
young cowboy and was rising slowly to his feet. He
dusted himself off and glanced at Jocko, who was a
red-cheeked tenderfoot, with a square face and blue
eyes. He looked humiliated and wiped the blood from
his mouth on his sleeve.

The crowd seemed to enjoy the sight, and watched
Slocum as he leaned down to give the cowboy a hand,
lifting him to his feet. Then Slocum turned to look at the
gleeful men, and the sight of something in his eyes
froze their laughter. They stood silent, watching Mul-

lins, wondering what he'd do. With a shrewd, calculating glance at Slocum, Mullins turned and went into the saloon. The men followed him.

Jocko watched silently, then turned to Slocum. "Sorry we got tangled. Not my fault."

"I know. Slocum's the name."

"Jock Collins." He reached into his pocket for a smoke.

Slocum watched him light up with an unsteady hand. "What made you tangle with that monster?"

Jock took a long draw from the cigarette and sat on the wood bar of the porch. "That monster was 'Muscles' Mullins. We were all talkin' about the killin' the other day." His grin was wry. "I said some things he didn't like, that he disagreed with."

Slocum smiled. "Mullins doesn't look like a man who's interested in disagreement."

"Especially about Slade," Jock said.

Slocum looked at him. "What about Slade?"

"You know him?"

"Not yet." He reached into his shirt pocket for a cigarillo. "What about Slade?"

"I disagreed. That's what riled Mullins. Slade shot Blake some days ago. Some of us were drinkin' and talkin' about it. I said it was a damned shame because Slade, who's a gunfighter, forced Blake to draw. He didn't want to fight. Wanted to back off."

Jock flipped the ash off his cigar. "But Slade is a friend of Mullins, and Mullins told me Blake was yellow, that he should have pulled his gun instead of being forced. And that I oughta mind my own business."

Jock looked at the dust on his pants and brushed it off. Slocum watched him with cool green eyes. "I reckon I had too much liquor in me to be careful, because I went on with it. I said a man has a right to fight or not. Pushing a man into an unequal fight is murder. That damned Slade, I said, is a gunfighter and a killer. Well, as I learned, Mullins is a friend of Slade, so he got riled and pushed me. I had had enough whiskey to cuss him. That's when he pummeled me and I went through the door."

Slocum nodded. "It's good to hear you were defending Tim Blake. Blake was a friend of mine."

"Well, Mullins didn't think much of him."

"Where is this Slade?" Slocum asked.

"Some say he's gone to Ledville." Jock flipped the cigarette suddenly and stood up.

"Where you goin'?" Slocum asked.

Jock looked uncertain. "Dunno."

"Let's go back in there," Slocum said. "Let me buy you a drink."

A slow smile twisted Jock's lip, and he winced from the pain. "Mullins wouldn't like that. And I don't like the idea of getting my face rearranged."

Slocum clapped his shoulder. "Don't worry about a thing. Let's go back in there."

"A mighty dangerous idea, Slocum."

Slocum shrugged. "Well, you can't let him buffalo you and lose your nerve. You can go back in and hold your head up. I'll be alongside you."

Jock Collins was startled at Slocum's proposition. He recognized the truth of Slocum's remark that not to go back in because he'd been thrown out by Mullins would be a failure of nerve. But who would blame him? Mullins had a mighty fist. Still, there was something about the lean, powerful stranger that calmed his fears. Jock had been roughed up and humiliated by Mullins. And it could be much worse this time. But if he went back into the Deadeye, he knew he'd feel good about himself, no matter what happened. And Slocum had told him not to worry, and he was inclined to believe him.

Jock managed a smile, though it hurt his mouth. "All right. I need a drink to ease the pain."

Slocum grinned. And, as they started for the batwing doors, he muttered, "Nothing to worry about, Jocko. You die only once."

That jolted Jock, so that when they walked through the doors, he had to work hard to bring his painful mouth into a smile.

The sounds of men drinking and gambling hit Slocum as he led the way to the bar. But when the men caught sight of him, especially of Jock, the sounds slowly simmered down, and the men looked at Jock, then at Mullins seated at a table, aware that this setup could be explosively entertaining.

Slocum took a space at the bar, with Jock alongside. The barman came up to them. He had a bald head with fringed hair on the sides and a heavy-jawed face with wise brown eyes which had seen much of life's excitements played out in his saloon.

"I'm Tully," the barman said. "What's your pleasure, mister?" he asked.

"Slocum's the name. Whiskey for me and my friend."

Tully's eyes slid to the table where Mullins sat with a big-bosomed lady. Then Tully slapped two glasses and a bottle on the bar. He turned to Jock. "Mister, there's nothing wrong with your guts. Can't say that much for your brains."

Slocum's glance was a touch severe. "Just put the whiskey down and take the money. That's your job."

Tully shrugged. "Just tryin' to keep the saloon from gettin' messed up with blood, Mr. Slocum."

A couple of men nearby laughed. Slocum turned to them. They looked solemn and turned away.

Slocum raised his glass, and Jock did likewise. He drew a deep breath. "That helps."

For the first time, Slocum turned slowly to face the saloon, as did Jock.

Mullins had been watching them, his eyes big and amazed. The last thing he expected was Jock back at the bar, drinking. He was convinced that, by himself, Jock would never have made so rash a decision, returning to the area of mayhem. He turned to the woman at his table, a blonde with big blue eyes and a wide red mouth.

"Some folks, Greta, are real thick-headed. Gotta punch some sense into their heads."

She said nothing, just stared with interest at the man with Jock Collins.

Mullins stood up, and the talk in the saloon became soft as the men watched. He sauntered up to Slocum and Jock. "I might be wrong about this, Jock, but I thought I threw you the hell outa here."

"When was that, Mullins?" Jock asked innocently.

Slocum smiled. Jock had got his nerve back nicely.

"When?" Mullins became truculent. "Just minutes ago."

Jock frowned as if trying to remember, but then shook his head. "Not sure of that."

Mullins grinned sadistically. "You got a fat lip and a mouthful of blood. That should remind you."

Jock raised his glass, drank, and said nothing, then cast a curious look at Slocum, who was calmly listening. For a nervous moment, Jock remembered that Slocum had said not to worry. Maybe he should.

Mullins was ignoring Slocum. "But if you forgot, Jock, I'm goin' to remind you. This time I'll take care you don't forget. Give you something to remember me by." He rolled up his shirt sleeve.

"Just a minute," said Slocum.

Mullins glared at him. "This ain't your fight, mister. But if you'd like to get into it, I'll be glad to knock out some of your teeth."

"I'm a peaceful man, Mullins," Slocum said. "What have you got against my friend Jock?"

"Whatever I got against him is none of your business. Stand aside while I give your *friend* a taste of bare knuckles."

"No, don't do that, Mullins. He's here as my guest. And I wouldn't like to see him mistreated."

Mullins studied him, and his massive features twisted into a grin. "I've got to say, like Jock here, you've got more guts than brains, mister. So step aside while I straighten out this mulehead here."

Slocum just shook his head, smiling. "I wouldn't do that, Mullins."

Mullins growled. "You must be loco, mister, steppin' into a fight that ain't yours. It's your funeral."

As Mullins spoke, with sudden trickery he shot a hard right at Slocum's chin, which, if it had hit true, would have put him to sleep. Instinctively, Slocum shifted and took the glancing blow on his cheek instead. Still, it jarred him from his head to the soles of his feet.

A look of sadistic pleasure swept over Mullins as he

noted it, and, grunting, he swung his left, aiming to finish off this nervy green-eyed stranger. But Slocum backed off to let his head clear. Mullins followed fast, swinging a right that to his surprise was blocked by an iron arm. He swung a left and felt *it* blocked too. He paused again, surprised, and that's when he saw the lightning punch come at his gut. It hit like the kick of a horse. Mullins bent over, leaving his jaw exposed. Slocum threw two hard blows, backed with the power of his shoulder. Mullins grunted in pain. He raged and lunged, throwing his fists in fury. Slocum caught one, and the pain of it jolted him. Mullins could put a man away with one punch. Slocum backed off, stayed light of foot, danced side to side, and ducked as Mullins threw wild punches. Then, stopping suddenly and planting his legs firmly, Slocum met Mullins as he again rushed forward slugging at his gut with rights and lefts. Mullins staggered, and for a moment his eyes blanked. Lightning fast, Slocum swung a powerful right at the man's chin with his back muscles behind the blow. Mullins stood still, wavered like an axed tree, then dropped in a heap to the floor. He lay there, inert.

There was an awed silence in the saloon. The drinkers had believed without doubt that the massive Mullins would make short work of Slocum and chop him to pieces. But in front of their amazed eyes the reverse had happened. The green-eyed stranger had made every punch count, and he had thunder in his fists. A burst of sound came from the drinkers.

Tully, used to the mop-up after fights, signaled to two men, who pulled Mullins to the back of the saloon. Then with a small smile Tully filled two glasses for Slocum and Jock. "Winner's drink, on the house."

Slocum lifted his whiskey glass, gulped it, then pulled a kerchief and put it to his cheek to blot the blood.

Jock lifted his drink and grinned. "I knew it'd be okay to come back if you swung along."

Slocum nodded, and his gaze swept the saloon. Always a good idea to be alert in case some friend of Mullins wanted vengeance. It looked all right, except for one cowboy in the corner of the bar, in a gray shirt and a black hat. His expression was not hostile but curious, almost friendly. He smiled. Slocum felt something familiar about him but couldn't pin it down. He expected that the cowboy might approach him, but at that moment a dust-covered man pushed open the swinging doors and yelled. "Hey, take a look out here!"

The men rushed to the doors, and Slocum heard their excitement. When he came out he saw the two dusty horses and the two dead men laid over the saddles.

Slocum moved closer, with Jock at his elbow, "That's Jaspers and Brown," said Jock. "Grant's gunmen. They were supposed to bring Slade back dead like that, but it looks like it happened the other way."

The men had been hit in front, no doubt about that. Beat at the draw? No way to know if Slade had hit them separately or both at one time. But he had mowed them down.

"Hit them straight on," said Jock, his voice awed. "Maybe both at once. He's fast."

Slocum nodded. If Slade had done that he had to be fast—and dangerous. So he shot the hell out of Jaspers and Brown. How would Grant take that? Slocum wondered. Grant didn't seem to be a man who liked to be beat at anything. Again, Slocum wondered how good Jaspers and Brown were. Did it matter?

Slade had shot Blake.

He turned to the dust-covered cowboy. "Where'd you pick them up, mister?"

"Halfway to Ledville. Lyin' flat out on the trail." He shook his head. "Thought they'd been ambushed by Apaches till I saw the horses grazin'. I loaded 'em and brought 'em here." His face was grim. "Figured Mr. Grant would want to know about his men."

"That was right, Lem," said a husky cowboy. "We'll take 'em up to the Grant ranch."

Slocum stroked his chin thoughtfully. Slade was out there on the trail to Ledville. He'd killed Tim Blake, and he might have some answers. Slocum walked to his horse. He'd start on the trail to Ledville in the morning.

The next morning Slocum stepped into Sara's Cafe to have breakfast before starting on the trail to Ledville. He sat at the table and Sara, a smiling rotund woman, came over. "You look like you need a man-sized breakfast," she said.

He reached up to his aching red, swollen cheek. "I'll have eggs, steak, biscuits, and coffee. Plenty of it. Need to restore my strength."

She was grinning. "Heard you upset our local fightin' champ."

Slocum smiled grimly. She went to the kitchen, and he began to think about Slade. The more he thought, the more he gritted his teeth.

He was chewing steak when he heard the clatter of horses' hooves, as four riders came up to the cafe. It was Grant and his three escorts.

He came in alone and stood in front of Slocum's table. "Mind if I join you?"

"Sit down."

"Bring some coffee, Sara," he told her.

Slocum studied Grant's rugged face, which looked composed. He had lost two men but he didn't seem riled. Slocum wondered if anything could upset a man like him.

His voice was calm and measured. "They tell me you gave Mullins a bad bruising." A small smile hovered about his lips. "That's good. Nobody ever did that to Mullins."

"Maybe I was lucky," Slocum said, touching his cheek tenderly. "He punches like a mule's kick."

"I think he knocked a mule on its ass once," Grant said. He paused, and a steely glint came to his gray eyes. "I lost two good men yesterday. Reckon you know that."

Slocum nodded.

Grant's mouth was hard. "I'm afraid we underestimated Slade. I'm not sure we've got any single gunfighter who can handle him." He stared at Slocum.

"Reckon I'm going to have to try."

Grant frowned. "To be honest, I'd hate to see you go up against him, Slocum. I know you want revenge for Tim."

Slocum kept eating.

Sara brought out the coffee for Grant. He lifted the cup and sipped it. Then he jerked his thumb at his three riders loafing outside the cafe. "I'm putting them on Slade. They'll work together. Each of them's a fast gun. They'll take care of him. Steele, the redhead out there, is a lightning gun."

Slocum glanced through the window. Steele wore a gray Stetson, a red neckerchief, and he looked tough and lean.

Grant went on. "I know you're just achin' to get Slade, but it might be smart to leave that job to these men. They want revenge for Jaspers and Brown, who were good friends."

Slocum drank his coffee, thinking that he didn't want to just shoot Slade, he wanted to find out why Slade shot Tim.

Grant smiled. "Of course, I can't stop you from hunting Slade down. I understand your feelings, that he shot Tim, your friend. But figure it like this—Slade gets a bullet. Does it matter whose bullet just as long as he's dead?"

Slocum wiped his lips. Grant was making a nice gesture. He figured he was saving Slocum the danger of a showdown with a deadly gunfighter.

"I appreciate your offer, Mr. Grant. But I'm after personal satisfaction."

Grant nodded. "You might want to work with my men. A posse like that would make sure that Slade's a dead man."

Slocum stood. "Real nice of you, Mr. Grant, but I work alone."

Grant followed him out of the cafe. "Slocum," he said, "I thought you oughta meet my boys. Steele, Lonnie, and Amos. Good men to have on your side."

They were hefty and hard-muscled, especially Steele, who looked every inch a gunfighter.

Slocum nodded. They nodded too but seemed detached, as if they didn't particularly care who he was. Steele, however, gave him a measured look.

Grant spoke easy. "I was figuring that Slocum would join you men, make a posse to trail and gun down Slade. But Slocum tells me he's a man who works alone."

He smiled, pulled out a cigar, and lit it. "So now we've got a contest—you men against Slocum to see who gets Slade first." He waved toward the west. "He's out there on the trail, or maybe in Ledville. He's a vicious gunslinger, and not afraid of anything. So you men ride out and let him know there's plenty to be afraid of."

Grant looked at them, then turned to his horse, swung over the saddle, and rode straight and strong up the street.

The men watched him silently. Then Steele turned to Slocum. "Ever met Slade?"

Slocum shook his head.

"He's mean, smart, and fast. Didn't surprise me that he mowed down Jaspers and Brown. We might have to hit him from more than one side. Sure you don't want to hitch up with us?"

Slocum studied the three men. Only Steele seemed interested in the hitch-up; the other two couldn't care less. He wondered why.

"Thanks a lot, Steele. Probably it's smart to team up, but it's my way to work alone. No offense, I hope."

Steele looked thoughtful. "None taken. So now it's goin' to be a race to see who gets to Slade first. Can't honestly say I wish you luck." He turned to Lonnie and Amos and said, "Let's go for Slade."

Slocum watched them mount up. As they started to ride, Steele threw a glance back at Slocum. The look was so strange that Slocum stood in his tracks almost half a minute before he moved to his horse. He swung over the roan and rode west for a while, thinking about Steele and the meaning of that look. If he had read it right, it had been anger—almost hate. Unless it was the way the sunlight struck his face. It was easy to twist the meaning of an expression hit by the sun.

Still, it was strange.

5

By the time Slocum, who was following the trail to Ledville, stopped to make coffee, the sky had darkened. Gray cloud masses, blown in by a north wind, blocked the sun. He could smell the threat of rain.

He started riding again, his keen eyes, as always, scrutinizing the land. Survival in the territory depended on how you read signs. He saw prints of rabbits and coyotes, then fresh hoofprints. Two were unshod, one shod: Apaches trailing a rider headed west.

He pushed the roan up a twisting trail until he reached a crest of the humpbacked mountains that gave a broad view of the land below. Amid thick brush, trees, and boulders he could see the two Apaches, probably renegades, off their horses, moving silently in a crouch toward a cowboy sitting at his campfire. Something looked familiar about the cowboy. Slocum was puzzled, but then he remembered the man in the black hat at the saloon who had smiled after Mullins had been knocked down.

As Slocum pulled out his rifle he wondered what the hell the cowboy was doing on this trail. How'd he get here so fast? What was his destination? Whatever it was, he'd never make it if he didn't get a sniff of the Apaches.

Slocum crouched behind a rock, studying the Apache moves.

The Apache slipped like wraiths from behind rock to brush, never moving until they felt it right. They were working to get close to the cowboy, who'd been eating out of a tin dish and now looked like he was dreaming.

Slocum's mouth tightened. In less than a minute the young man would be a goner. Slocum raised his rifle. Then, to his astonishment, the cowboy came alive, making perfect moves: his gun spit fire to the left, dropping one Apache. As the cowboy rolled, the other Apache fired, just missing but revealing his position. Flat on his stomach, the cowboy fired again. The Apache grabbed his side and lurched back toward his spotted pony.

The cowboy stayed crouched behind a low boulder, and, though he heard the pony move, he did nothing. Neither did Slocum. Slouched, the cowboy came forward, found the dead Apache, gazed at him for a moment, then went back to his camp. He threw his things in his saddlebag, swung over his horse, and rode west on the trail to Ledville.

Slocum scratched his chin. That hombre sure seemed to be in a hurry. He scanned the land carefully as he came down the incline to look at the dead Apache. He was husky, smooth-skinned, with a broad face and sightless black eyes. It was common for renegade Apaches to prey on wandering drifters and settlers. Slocum walked to the camp and looked at it. Again, he wondered how the cowboy had got out here this quick. He must have started last night—but why?

Slocum's keen hearing picked up a delicate movement of brush, and his gun jumped. He heard a grunt, then the sound of a body as it fell.

The second Apache. He'd come back for his comrade, to help or to bury him. Apache braves rarely abandoned their comrades. He had spotted Slocum and figured on a touch of revenge against the hated white man.

Slocum pulled out his shovel and buried the two Apaches in the same grave.

As he rode toward Ledville, his mind fastened on the cowboy in the black hat. No slouch with the gun; he sure had been smart, playing possum against the tracking Apaches. Who was he? Why'd he look familiar, reminding him of someone?

This trail took a man to Ledville and maybe to Slade. And somewhere back of him, Steele and his two boys were on it.

Could Slade be the target for this cowboy, too?

A most wanted desperado, this Slade. Were they all after his hide? Did they all want him dead?

But Slocum wanted him alive. Dead men told you nothing.

Slocum raced for a nearby rock shelter as a quick, fierce rainstorm swept down, wiping out tracks. After the rain eased, a strong wind drove the clouds east, leaving the skies clear and sunny.

Half a mile out of Ledville, a shoe loosened on the roan. Slocum walked the horse into town, reaching it just before sundown. There were plenty of cowboys and townfolk moving around the main street. He felt edgy, wondering if Steel and his boys had beat him here.

He brought the horse to Kerry's Livery. The muscular smith looked at the roan's hooves.

"Needs a new shoe, mister."

"Slocum's the name. Do them all."

Kerry nodded lightly. "A fine horse." He ran his hand over the roan's great chest and strong legs.

"Heart of gold," Slocum said. He lit a cigarillo. "Any strangers come into town?"

"They come and they go. Some get planted here." Kerry's smile was wry.

"Looking for a man called Slade."

Kerry's face was grim as he patted the sleek back of the roan. He cleared his throat. "You a lawman?"

Slocum shook his head.

"You look like one," Kerry said. "Reckon your business with Slade is none of my business. But he'd be the last man I'd tangle with."

"Why so?"

Kerry nodded. "In the saloon last night a stranger bucked Slade about a poker play. Just like that. Slade hadn't been drinkin' much and was tryin' to be peaceful. The stranger figured Slade gutless and got ornery. Slade shot the cowboy's gun hand, then shot his other hand, too. That tamed him—stopped his cardplaying, too."

Kerry stroked his jaw. "He's a streak, Slade is." He measured Slocum. "Yup, were it me, I'd steer clear of Slade. Nothin' hurts more than to see a good man gunned down in the prime of life."

Slocum thought of Tim Blake and hitched up his gunbelt. "It's a sad thing. And keeps happening to good men." He walked to the door. "Take good care of my horse."

Kerry nodded thoughtfully. Slocum was a good man, bucking trouble. He wondered if he'd ever get back to his fine horse.

Slocum sauntered up the street, which was busy with citizens shopping before the stores closed. He walked past the wooden shacks until he reached the saloon. It was big, smoky, with plenty of drinkers and some women.

He ordered whiskey, took the bottle and glass to a table, sat down, and gazed at the men.

He suddenly realized that he had no idea of what Slade looked like. The saloon was crowded, with husky, mean-looking cowboys, and Slade could be one of them. Well, he didn't know what Slade looked like, but then Slade didn't know him, either.

The men were red with drink and ornery. The women were busty, in low-cut, silky, flouncy dresses. One of them, with a pretty doll's face, round blue eyes, and sensual lips, was looking at him.

He was beginning to perk up when the doors pushed open and a cowboy stood there, staring at the men. Slocum, to his surprise, recognized Lonnie, one of the two men with Steele. His face was tight, his eyes hard as they swept over the drinkers, then widened when he found what he was looking for. *Slade!*

Lonnie's hand streaked to his gun.

Not long after Slocum had reached Ledville, Steele, Lonnie, and Amos were also approaching the town.

As Steele rode, he thought about Slade. He didn't know if he'd find him at the saloon, but he did know he was hungry, and he figured it'd be a good idea to stop at the town cafe before going after Slade. Steele liked his comforts, liked to take care of them before he did business. And he knew what his business was—Grant had told him to make sure and kill Slade. His mind worked on that.

But he couldn't help think also about Slocum. That Slocum! Steele thought he was one mangy dog. When Grant asked Slocum to join a posse to track Slade, Slocum had said he liked to work alone. Steele's mouth tightened. A loner. Loners were dangerous. You didn't know what they were thinking.

Perched on a rise, Steele could see the town, its shacks sprawled out under the descending sun. A town in Arizona, like many in the territory, but this one held the mystery.

Steele thought about Slocum again. He looked like a fast smart gunfighter. Steele knew plenty about gunfighters—he made his living as one, and you didn't survive in that occupation if you didn't know what you were doing. Steele had made a study of fast gunmen, and he found the best were built lean, quick to sense danger, quick to shoot first.

Steele knew about guns, too, how you wore them to

draw fast, how to get a hairline trigger, how to draw with the sun in your opponent's eyes if you could. The more you knew, the longer you lasted in an occupation that had a built-in short life expectancy.

Steele also knew Slade—a Tombstone gunfighter with steady nerves and a flash draw. Steele didn't like him, never had. He didn't know if he could outdraw Slade, something he hoped not to find out. There were safer ways to take care of a mangy dog.

Steele rode his horse toward the cafe. He'd stop there first. You couldn't shoot a man easy on an empty stomach. He clamped his teeth as his mind continued to work on gunfighters. The trouble with them, was they were always testing to see how good they were. That was the danger. You pitted yourself against a famous gun like Billy the Kid or Doc Holliday or Kid Cassidy. If you beat them, it gave you a big rep. They talked about you in saloons from Kansas to Texas. And fame was sweet to every gunfighter.

Steele could see the cafe and, further down the street, the saloon. Would Slade be in there? Might be smart to check. And what about Slocum? Steele's lips tightened. That polecat was a mystery. Hard to know about a man like him. He looked dangerous. You sensed it in the way he walked, the way he was built. And those green, piercing eyes seemed to reach into your skull for what you were thinking. Steele smiled grimly. What would Slocum give to figure out his thoughts? He might be smart but he was no mind reader.

The sky was flaming red and orange, a brilliant sunset by the time the three men reached the cafe. Steele drooled at the thought of steak and fritters, pecan pie and coffee. He looked at the other end of the street at the two-story saloon.

He turned to Lonnie. "We need a square meal. Why don't you take a quick look in the saloon and see if Slade or Slocum is there. Don't do anything. Just look, come back, and tell us."

Lonnie nodded.

Steele swung off his sorrel and brushed at his dusty pants and vest. Amos did likewise. They both stood there, watching Lonnie ride toward the saloon.

Then they went into the cafe.

Lonnie, a hefty, brown-eyed gunman, liked the idea of riding up to the saloon alone. He knew Slade, the boys knew him, they knew he could draw. Lonnie couldn't help thinking what a prize it would be if he did see Slade and nailed him on the spot. He glowed at the idea, though he suspected it might not be wise. But he'd done his share of gunfighting and was still around to talk about it. You could be good, but until you knocked out a top gun you didn't know how good you were.

Damn, what a prize if he could pick off Slade. See him, surprise him, shoot him. He tingled with excitement as he swung off his horse, threw the reins at the rail post, walked up the two steps to the batwing doors, and pushed them open. His eyes swept the crowd. There he was—Slade!

His hand flashed down to his holster, but before he could draw, a bullet hit his chest and he arched back and plummeted through the door and lay flat out, his gun unfired in his hand. Lonnie's eyes were still open. Thoughts flashed through his brain like a thousand lights popping. His life. Now he was going to die, in probably a minute. Why? Because he'd wanted to be a hero. If only he had listened to Steele. If . . . if . . . that's how you died, you took the wrong "if."

Men looking down at Lonnie saw his eyes go empty.

The gunfighter who had shot him, a taut, powerful man with a lean, hawklike face and glittering black eyes, was standing two tables away from Slocum.

Though he looked dangerous, his voice and manner were surprisingly mild. "You all saw it. I didn't do a thing. He pulled his pistol."

The gunfighter struck a lucifer, relit his cigarillo, then grinned widely. "But he *was* a mite slow."

There was soft, appreciative laughter from some men.

His black gleaming eyes swept the saloon, as if checking for a challenger. For a moment his eyes flickered to Slocum, but then he seemed satisfied. He puffed his cigarillo.

"That's right, Slade," said one red-faced cowboy, eager to please the gunfighter. "That coyote jerked his gun first."

"But he sure ruined my taste for drinkin'," Slade said. He sauntered to the doors, peered into the street, then, finding it clear, he pushed through with never a glance at the dead Lonnie.

Slocum lifted his drink. So that was Slade. A deadly hawk, a killer, yet capable of talking easy.

The pretty doll had spotted him and was headed his way. He wondered what action to take. The doll or Slade? He walked to the door. Slade had mounted up and was riding east. Toward Black Rock? He'd be out on the trail this night. Easy to track. He'd catch up with Slade.

He felt the doll's breast brush up against his arm. "What's the hurry, cowboy? The fun's in here." He looked at her pretty face, her sensual mouth, her yellow-brown eyes glowing with the promise of excitement. Yes, the fun was here. Slade would leave a trail.

He felt horny.

Upstairs she brought her face to his and he kissed her pretty lips. She put her arms around him, holding tight, pressing her curvy body against his. Then she turned him loose.

"I'm Lori," she said, pulling her dress over her shoulders. Her full, rounded breasts popped into view. Her brown nipples were already erect. She had a nice, sensual body, with a flat stomach, fine thighs, and long legs. Slocum felt his flesh surge. She looked fascinated at the sight of his vitality and reached for it. Then she began to pleasure him. He watched her for a while. Then he put his tongue to her breast and stroked the curve of her silky buttocks. Her breathing came fast. She squeezed tightly against him, then pulled him back to the bed and over her. Her thighs came apart, and he was pitched high when he entered her. She grabbed him, thrusting hard. Again he paused to caress her breasts, the erect nipples. Their bodies started to move together with strong rhythm, and his pleasure sharpened. He thrust hard, and she came up to meet him. The tension became urgent, and he began to drive fiercely— it left her gasping. Suddenly she tightened and groaned. Holding hard to her buttocks, he drove repeatedly until the final release.

After they had dressed, they sat relaxing over drinks. "So what are you doing in town, Slocum?"

"Hunting for a man called Slade."

She stared at him. "Slade? That could be mighty dangerous. You saw what happened downstairs. He's deadly."

Slocum shrugged.

"Why are you after him?" she asked.

"He shot a good friend of mine."

"A good friend? Who?"

"Tim Blake."

An odd expression came over her face. "Tim Blake, from Black Rock?"

Slocum's lips tightened. "Did you know Tim?"

"I knew him, yes."

Slocum studied her.

She smiled. "Oh, he dropped around when he came to town."

Slocum chewed his lip. "You mean he saw you?"

"Maybe." She ran her hands over her breasts.

Slocum frowned as he grappled with a new side of Blake. "Why the hell would he do that to his wife? She's beautiful."

She shrugged. "Wouldn't be the first man to do that to his wife."

He stared at Lori, a pretty young hussy, a sporting girl. "And you know Slade?" he asked.

"Yes."

Slocum thought of the hawk-faced hombre with the fast gun that he'd seen downstairs. "He shot Tim Blake. Did he maybe talk about that? Why he did it?"

"No."

Thoughtfully, Slocum lit a cigarillo. "What the hell

would Slade have against Tim? A decent hombre. Tim didn't want a showdown."

She lifted the whiskey glass to her lips and sipped it. "Slade is a moody cowboy. Can be nice, but give him a coupla drinks and he turns mean as a rattlesnake. As soon kill you as look at you."

Slocum was tired of hearing that. He said, "But Tim was easy, he wasn't pushing for a fight."

She shook her head. "When Slade feels mean, he just wants to shoot to get the meanness out. Probably Blake happened to be in the wrong place at the wrong time."

Slocum blew smoke at the ceiling. It could be just that, he thought. Slade was a mangy snake with a poison bite when he felt mean. That was all it was. He looked at Lori. "Do you know Midge Blake?"

Lori's lips tightened, and she drank the rest of her whiskey. "I've seen her in Black Rock. Snooty lady. And butter wouldn't melt in her mouth."

"What the hell does that mean?"

Lori just shrugged.

"She's pregnant."

"So what. Doesn't make her holy. Getting pregnant is what women do."

Slocum's mouth tightened. He didn't like to hear cheap things said about Midge. He stared at Lori. A doll's face and a lovely body.

He stood up. "Well, Lori, you're a good screw, but you've got a viper's tongue. I've wasted enough time here."

He went toward the door.

"Slade will get you," she said.

•   •   •

Steele was in the cafe drinking coffee. He felt uneasy. Where in hell was Lonnie? By this time he should have been back from the saloon.

Steele's face screwed with thought. Had that polecat stopped to guzzle? He might, if Slade wasn't there.

But suppose he was there.

Again that nasty feeling. Steele's hand gripped the cup hard. Had he made a mistake in sending Lonnie? That mulebrain sometimes imagined himself a great gunfighter. Would he be crazy enough to tackle Slade if he was there?

A sense of foreboding came over Steele. It hadn't occurred to him that Lonnie might dream he was good enough to outdraw Slade.

He stopped eating and looked at Amos, brawny and thick-necked, who kept stuffing his face with chili, never pausing a moment to wonder about his sidekick, Lonnie.

Steele put down his coffee cup. "Let's go."

Amos stared at him, fork in hand. "But I ain't finished eatin' yet, Steele."

Had to stuff himself with his lousy chili. "What about Lonnie?" Steele asked.

"What d'ya mean?"

"Where the hell is he? Should be here by now."

Amos's face creased with thought. "He's havin' shots at the saloon."

"Shots? Yeah, probably *tryin'* shots at Slade."

Amos's eyes opened wide at the thought. "At Slade? D'ya think he's dumb enough? He couldn't beat Slade in a year."

Steele's mouth tightened. "He's dumb enough. And by now he might have found that out."

He stood up, and Amos followed close behind him.

In the street Steele looked toward the saloon. Outside under the big bright moon he saw two men loading a body on a wagon. He walked toward it, his eyes narrowing as for one hopeful moment he imagined it might be Slade. If Lonnie got a surprise shot at Slade, that might work. A slender hope, because if Lonnie had beat Slade, he would have been back to the cafe, boasting.

Coming nearer, Steele saw the bloody vest, and a quiver went through him. Lonnie. Stone dead. He glanced at Amos, staring hard-faced at the body in the wagon, the chest bloody, the eyes vacantly open.

He came up to the men and spoke to the grizzled old-timer, probably the burying man. "What happened here?" he asked.

The old-timer shook his head. "Don't know who he is. Came into the saloon and whipped out his gun. But a mite too slow, Slade said."

Steele felt anger. That mulebrain, Lonnie, dreaming himself a great gunfighter, had tried to draw against Slade. "Slade in there now?"

"He's gone."

"Not there, eh. Know where's he headed?" He smiled sourly. "Got business with him."

The man stared at him curiously, as if visualizing business for Boot Hill. "Wouldn't know, mister. He just walked out the saloon after the shootin', just like that."

Steele turned to Amos. "Let's go in there."

"Why?"

"Maybe Slocum's in there."

"If he had been there, he'd be shooting."

"Let's go in and find out somethin'."

They went in, walked to the short end of the bar, and stood there while Steele studied the men. Mean-looking mongrels mostly, but no Slocum. Then he saw Lori sitting with a bald-headed, sinewy cowboy. He walked over and sat at the table.

She looked at him without enthusiasm and jerked her finger at the bald man. "My friend, Joel. Joel, this is Steele."

The bald cowboy looked at the rugged, hard-eyed gunman, shrugged, stood up, and walked to the bar, facing the table.

Frowning slightly, Lori fluffed her hair. "What's on your mind, Steele? You don't look fun-minded."

"No. Just saw a friend of mine. Dead."

She sighed. "That's how it happens, Steele. Here today, dead tomorrow."

"Not funny," he growled. "Did you see it?"

"We all saw it. He came in, pulled his gun, and got shot. In three seconds."

"By Slade?"

"Yeah, Slade."

Steele brooded again on the stupidity of Lonnie. Then he said, "Happen to know where Slade was headed?"

She shook her head.

Steele's mouth tightened. If Slade was going east, he'd be headed back to Black Rock. He had to know that. He didn't want to lose time.

Then he thought of something. "Happen to know a man named Slocum?" That hit her, he was sure. She stared at him.

"Reckon you did." He showed his teeth. From the gleam in her eye, Steele figured she had got Slocum on her mattress.

"Yeah, Slocum was here."

"And he saw the shootin'?" Steele's voice was vicious.

"Everyone saw it."

"Where's he now?"

"Gone."

"I can see that." He leaned forward, his voice intense, almost threatening. "Which way did Slocum go?"

Lori glanced toward the bar at Joel, who had been watching them sharp-eyed. Steele, aware he might not get the truth, reached into his pocket and put a gold coin on the table.

"Which way, honey. East or west?"

"West."

Her hand went out for the coin, but Steele got there first.

"Goin' to lie, weren't you? I'll just keep this money. You oughta tell the truth without being paid for it."

She scowled. "You cheapskate. It ain't your job to teach morals."

He stood up, grinning. "That's right, honey. Tell you what, Lori. Next time I come to town, I'll treat your ass extra good."

Her lip curled. "You'll never get near my ass, cheapskate."

He laughed and started for the door. When he got to the bar, the mustached cowboy, Joel, stepped in front of him. "You givin' our sweet little Lori trouble, mister?"

Steele's mouth tightened. "Just move to the side, cowboy."

Joel's mustache quivered with sudden rage. He swung at Steele's jaw, connected, and Steele went barreling back. As he hit the floor, his gun came out and spit a bullet. It hit Joel's shoulder, spinning him around.

He fell and went for his gun. Steele shot it from his hand.

"Be glad you're breathin', mister," Steele growled again. And still holding his gun, with Amos alongside, he went out of the saloon.

As they ran for their horses, Steele grunted at Amos, "Slocum's gone west after Slade. Slade might be goin' back to Black Rock. We gotta nail him. Grant wants Slade dead. We gotta be right on target this time. No mistakes."

6

The moon was a lonely ball of light in the night sky, casting silver beams on the sleeping earth.

Slade, the feared gunfighter, could see the moonlight strike the huge mountain as he and his pinto headed west.

He pointed the horse toward the high ground, looking for a nook for the night. Also, he wanted to study the land behind him. It wouldn't be surprising if someone was on his tail, considering what had happened at the saloon: Lonnie breaking in and pulling his gun. It meant that Steele and Amos were nearby. The unholy three. These three always clustered around Grant like watchdogs, and now he had turned them loose to tear his throat out if they could.

There was no doubt in Slade's mind that Steele was on his trail. That Grant wanted him dead. What astonished Slade was that Lonnie alone would draw against him. That unholy three were tricky. They never hit a man straight. But for some odd reason, Lonnie had come without the other two and tried for a quick shot. He had taken a chance: you spotted your man and shot him before he spotted you. Slade smiled, and in the moonlight his hawklike face looked more than ever like a bird of prey. He'd never turn his back on a door. Not the kind of life he had lived. Gunfighters didn't last long if they didn't calculate their chances. They had too many enemies—the kin of men they had killed, for instance. Any man could be a killer; you had to look in his eyes, dig in his mind, ferret out his feelings.

Slade knew this. That's why he had faced the door. He saw Lonnie the moment he stuck his head in, saw his eyes. He was there for killing. And Grant had sent him.

That's why he was headed back to Black Rock.

Slade's face reddened with rage as he thought of the wealthy rancher. He'd pay him off somehow.

By this time, Slade had climbed to a good height. He swung off the pinto and walked over to the jutting rock that gave a long view of the valley.

He studied the land. Then, in the strong moonlight, he finally saw the movements of small objects. He studied them.

More than one rider on his trail. What did it mean? Were they after him, or just riders headed for Black Rock? He didn't know, but whoever they were, they weren't going to catch him napping. First you cleaned out the yellowbellies, then you took sleeping time. He smiled. The polecat wasn't born yet who could pick him off.

Or draw a faster gun.

He was the fastest damned gun in Tombstone.

And he'd get back to Black Rock somehow and make Grant spit blood.

He sat down, cross-legged, cradling his rifle, and watched the small objects as approaching him became bigger.

Slocum pulled on his roan and looked up the rocky incline. Stones gleamed in the moonlight, and deep shadows under the stunted trees looked menacing. He'd been tracking Slade for hours and had good reason to believe he was up there, either camped for the night or waiting with a rifle for his tracker.

Slade had to know he was being tracked, Slocum felt. A rider who moved to such steep ground had to be protecting himself. And in this strong moonlight, he could see plenty.

For Slocum the trick was to get up there without getting shot down.

He swung off the roan, breathing deeply of the tangy air, and studied the climbing land in front of him. There were patches of thick brush, scattered rocks, and stunted trees, but still, it was risky. If he climbed, it would give Slade the odds—he had only to wait for his tracker to expose himself and then fire.

Slocum chewed his lip. Better to wait till morning, when Slade would ride on to Black Rock. He'd be more vulnerable on the trail.

He turned and stared at the land behind him. Two horses were coming—it had to be Steele and Amos, but why were they riding hell-bent for leather? Maybe because they were in a rage about Lonnie. Steele was vin-

dictive and fired up for revenge. He was out to squash
Slade as fast as possible.

Slocum rubbed his chin. If only they weren't determined to kill Slade on sight, he'd join them. Then Slocum remembered Steele's odd hostile look at him, back
in Black Rock, just before he rode off with his men.
Was it wise to trust an hombre who had looked at him
with such malevolence, momentary though it was. He
could think of no reason why Steele should be hostile
toward him—he didn't know Steele from a cactus. Slocum shrugged. In the war for survival in the territory, it
was always wiser to trust your feelings than your logic.
He decided to wait and try to persuade Steele not to
shoot that bastard Slade right off. Not till he squeezed
the truth out of him.

He positioned himself at a boulder; he never stood
where he'd be a target for a hidden gunman.

They had seen him, and Steele waved. They kept
coming, bent low on their horses, as if aware that under
a bright moon they might be in danger from a rifleman
perched on the rocky incline.

Slocum quietly smoked until they reached him. They
came off their horses, which were breathing hard after
the long run.

Steele stared at the incline, his face grim. "Is he up
there?"

"Wouldn't be surprised."

Steele pulled out a cigar and lit it. He turned to
Amos. "The whiskey."

Amos walked to his horse, pulled a whiskey bottle
from his saddlebag, and passed it to Steele.

Steele took a swig, then grinned at Slocum. "I guess
you're ready to work with us now." He didn't wait for

an answer, but went on. "That's smart. Reckon you know what happened to Lonnie."

Slocum nodded.

"That was one damned mulehead. I told him just to look in the saloon and do nothing. But he pulled his gun."

Steele raised the whiskey bottle to his lips, drank, and wiped his mouth with his sleeve. He stared hard at Slocum. "They tell me you were there. One question keeps comin' up. If you were there, how come you were sitting in the Deadeye with Slade and not pullin' your gun?"

Slocum calmly puffed at his cigarillo. "It's like this, Steele, I didn't know Slade was there. Didn't know what the hell he looked like. The way I found out was after he jerked his gun and shot Lonnie."

Steele thought about it and looked grim. "And after he shot Lonnie, *after*. Why didn't you shoot?"

Slocum smiled slowly. "Slade still had his gun out."

Steele took another swig, his eyes steady on Slocum, then he passed the bottle to Amos, who walked back to the saddlebag. "Then you stopped for a bit of play with Lori."

Slocum raised his eyebrows. So that's how Steele had figured out his trail. He'd talked to Lori. He flipped his cigarillo against a rock. "Listen, Steele. I'm ready to join you and hit Slade. But I don't want him dead. I want him talking' *before* he's dead."

Steele's eyes slitted. "Talkin'? About what?"

"I'm mighty curious why Slade shot my friend Tim Blake. Especially when Tim didn't want the draw."

Steele glanced at Amos, still at his horse, then back

to Slocum. "You ain't ever goin' to find that out, mister."

Slocum stared at him and started for his gun.

"Hold it." Steele raised his hands above his head. His voice was cold. "Look behind you."

He threw a glance behind him. Amos, smirking, was pointing his Colt.

Steele's eyes were icy. "No, Slocum, it doesn't look like you're goin' to do much talking to Slade." He brought his hands down to rub his chin thoughtfully. "I had been hopin' you'd help me get rid of Slade—before we pulled the gun on you. Reckon it's not to be."

Slocum's mouth hardened. Then he'd been right: that look on Steele's face had been hostile. He'd just been playing for time, hoping to get his help to bring down Slade. Then he'd try to put a bullet in his back, like now. That mangy dog Amos had got behind him, pretending to put the whiskey in his saddlebag.

Things looked real bad.

He scowled. "I don't remember doing you any harm."

Steele smiled. "Naw, you never did. I've got nothing against you, except you shoulda helped Lonnie."

He motioned for Amos, still holding his gun, to come alongside him, in front of Slocum. "I hate to see a man shot in the back," Steele said, grinning.

Slocum growled. "Why in hell are you doin' this, Steele?"

"Good question. Reckon you'll take it to hell with you. Maybe get the answer there."

Slocum knew he'd have to go for his gun and chance that Amos's bullet wouldn't kill him.

Steele nodded to Amos, who grinned widely and

slowly raised his Colt to aim at Slocum's heart. The crack of a rifle shot bounced off the crags. Amos jumped as his brains spewed from his head.

It was a paralyzing moment; then Slocum and Steele, realizing what had happened, ducked and went for their guns. Slocum's bullet hit Steele's chest dead center and he barreled back. A red stain started to spread against his shirt.

Slocum stayed flat aginst the boulder, shielded from gunfire, trying to figure it out.

His first thought was that Slade had fired from the rise. But Amos had been hit from behind. The rifle bullet had come from someone below, on the trail, a sharpshooter who'd been following Steele and Amos, probably from Ledville.

Who the hell would that be?

And why'd he shoot?

Peering down, Slocum just caught a glimpse of a black-hatted rifleman slipping behind rocks, going for his horse. The figure was familiar, and Slocum knew who it was. He'd seen him first in the Black Rock saloon. He'd seen him on the road to Ledville when he shot the Apaches. This was him again, doing sharpshooting riflework.

So who the hell was he? He'd been protective. From the beginning Slocum felt him to be friendly. Yet he seemed to steer clear of contact. Why didn't he come up if he was friendly? What was his game? He seemed to be always traveling either in front of, or behind him. Before Black Rock. After Ledville. Who was he tracking? Steele? Slade? Or himself? It wasn't dead certain that he had friendly intentions. But he was a hell of a sharpshooter. If he wanted Steele dead too, why didn't he shoot again? Maybe he had no clear shot or maybe he expected him to beat Steele. The rifleman had done his job—he had put Amos down to set up an even draw between Steele and him.

So what was his game? Who the hell knew the answer? Until he came forward, there was no way to know.

Slocum now thought of Slade. What was he doing while all this was happening? The firing had to make him a bit nervous. Was he still up there? Gone? Changed his position?

It was still risky to climb under this bright moon. He'd sweat out the night and in the morning go for Slade. He'd be on the trail to Black Rock by then.

He looked at the dead men sprawled on the ground. They might have been helpful in hunting Slade down, but now he'd have to do it alone.

Then he thought of Steele. "I've got nothing against you," he had said. But he was going to kill him anyway.

There's more here than meets the eye, Slocum thought. It was a barrel of snakes.

But maybe Slade had some answers.

The next morning the sun cast a rosy glow over the sawtoothed mountain, and the earth looked green and fresh. Slocum glanced about with pleasure, then made breakfast. As he drank his coffee he ruminated.

What stuck most in his mind was Steele's casual remark: "I've got nothing against you, except you shoulda helped Lonnie."

So why the guns?

Because he hadn't helped Lonnie? No way he could

have. That dumb polecat came through the door, pulled his gun, and got blasted.

No, something else was going on. Because Steele seemed to first want his help to nail Slade. After that he too would be the target for Steele's gun.

So what did it mean?

Slocum tried to put it together and began to wonder if it all came back to Grant.

It had been Grant who had ordered Steele and his two henchmen to kill Slade. Why? Revenge for Tim Blake? Or as a favor to Midge Blake? Or was there some other reason? But did he give Steele secret orders to kill him too? What the hell for? Grant, a courtly, generous rancher, with a fine reputation. What the hell was going on?

Slocum scratched his head. Even before Black Rock, back in Bitter Creek, and on the trail, gunmen were throwing bullets at him. Was all this part of some game to knock him off? And who was behind that?

It didn't seem possible. It had to be coincidental, and he was trying to sew them together.

And what about the rifleman who shot the hell out of Amos at the right moment, saving his life? Why'd he do that? And where in hell did he ride?

Slocum sighed heavily and finished his coffee.

There was nothing he could do now except go after Slade. Maybe *he* knew something.

Slade was a rare breed of gunman. Fast as hell. If he could only get close to that coyote. He had killed Tim, and he had to pay in blood. But Slade knew he was being tracked. And he was a killer who'd shoot on sight.

As Slocum put his gear into his saddlebag and swung over the roan, he decided it was going to be one helluva game, trying to get an answer out of Slade.

He nudged the roan up the incline, past the rocks and stunted trees. Although he believed that Slade was long gone, he moved with caution. Finally he reached Slade's camp, and, studying the tracks, he believed that Slade had some idea of the fracas below. From the droppings of his pinto, Slade wasn't far ahead.

The sun climbed, and the sky became cloudless and clear blue. After a mile of riding, Slade's trail went into a green valley and took convoluted twists through a densely wooded area—a risky stretch of land, the sort that a canny trailsman might use to bushwhack his tracker.

Slocum felt edgy and moved carefully. His instinct for danger kept him nervy.

It happened as he was puzzling over the tracks.

"Don't pull your gun, mister."

The calm voice had come from behind him, from a rock nearby. He had glanced at it, but believed it much too flat to conceal a man's body.

He'd been mistaken.

He stood transfixed, aware that he'd been outfoxed.

"Turn slow."

Slocum turned and saw Slade behind the flat rock, dirt on his clothes. He had dug a ditch below the rock, which enabled him to hide his body down under it, an old Apache trick.

Slade stood there, seemingly casual. He had not drawn his gun, as if he had complete confidence that he could beat any draw.

"Who the hell are you?" Slade asked.

"Slocum's the name."

Slade came toward him, his step casual, a man absolutely unafraid, sure of his gun speed. He stopped ten feet from Slocum. In the sunlight, the yellow-brown eyes in his hawklike face burned hard at Slocum. "You been trackin' me."

Slocum nodded.

Slade smiled curiously. "You, Steele, and his mangy sidekicks."

Slocum spoke slowly. "Steele and Amos. They wanted your hide."

Slade's face twisted with bizarre humor. "Don't see 'em anymore."

"No, not anymore."

"You shot Steele last night?" Slade's voice was measured, but he looked mobilized, ready to strike like a rattler, given the hint of a move.

Slocum kept his body immobile. He just nodded.

Finally Slade spoke. "You gotta be good if you beat Steele." He stroked his chin. "So they're all dead— Steele and his two mangy coyotes."

"Yes."

"Mighty strange if you were *all* trackin' me. Why'd you draw against Steele?"

" 'Cause he's a yellow dog," Slocum said.

Slade laughed. "That he is." He stared curiously. "Don't know a thing about you, Slocum, except that you been trackin' me." He paused, then his voice was low, flat. "Reckon I'm goin' to have to kill you."

Slocum cleared his throat. "Just tell me this, Slade. Why'd you shoot Tim Blake?"

"Blake?" Slade's eyes glittered. "So you're here because of Blake?"

Slocum nodded. "He didn't want a draw. You forced him. And his wife is goin' to have a baby."

Slade nodded. "I'll tell you, mister. Some joker paid me fifty dollars to shoot the hell outa Blake. That's why."

"Who was that joker?"

Slade smiled gently. "It ain't goin' to do you much good to know, Slocum, 'cause you're goin' to be dead in ten seconds." He bared his teeth in a strange smile, and his hawk's face looked deadly as he slipped into the gunfighter's crouch.

Slocum, too, was in the crouch, aware that he faced a top gun. His every nerve was alert, for death quivered on the razor edge of a second. He studied the yellow-brown eyes where the brain's signal would flash to the fingers.

The land about them seemed to sense the presence of death, and everything froze.

A bird started up from the nearby tree, and they streaked lightning fast for their guns. Both firing, the sound like one, but it was two, and Slade stood still, a smile on his face. It stayed there as he pitched forward on the ground, a bullet in his forehead.

Slocum wrenched with pain. Slade's bullet had bit his left arm, tearing a piece of flesh. He walked forward slowly.

Slade's smile was fixed on his face, and he'd carry it to hell with him.

Then Slocum thought of Tim. He'd be resting easy now—this bastard was paid off for him. But that didn't finish it. There was more ahead. He pulled out his shovel, and while he dug he thought: There was some joker behind Slade. Behind Steele. He was the real killer. But how to find him? It wasn't going to be easy. Who was it? Why in hell did he want Slade dead?

And why *him*?

The joker had a lot to answer for.

Slocum took his whiskey bottle from his saddle bag and pulled on it. He poured some over his wound and bound it. The sun was hot now. He wiped a film of sweat off his brow. His jaw clenched as he swung over the saddle and started on the trail back to Black Rock.

7

It was sundown when Slocum reached the outskirts of Black Rock. The sun sat on the horizon, a huge smoldering ball of fire, and the sky looked like a crimson sea.

Slocum rode out to the Blake ranch. He stopped at high ground to look down at it. Not much of a spread, but it did have a fine stream.

Riding to the ranch house, he couldn't help compare how things looked before, when he had ridden from it.

There was Slade, a cold-blooded gunfighter who had provoked and brutally shot Tim Blake. And there were Steele and his two sidekicks ordered to hunt down and shoot Slade.

All were dead.

He alone had come back from the war, somewhat hurt but not entirely out of the woods.

The trouble was he had no hard evidence that someone was behind these men. Only Slade's strange comment that he'd been paid to shoot Tim. Was he serious or clowning? Slade, who believed his gun was invincible, didn't care what he said, since he didn't believe Slocum was going anywhere.

Slocum smiled grimly. Seems Slade was positive but mistaken. In his experience, Slocum never met a gunman who believed he'd come out second best in a draw. And every time a gunfighter won a draw, it supported his secret belief that he was invincible.

He put the roan into a trot and soon reached the corral, where two cowboys were lounging. He didn't know them. He swung off the horse. They stared at him—a red-cheeked tenderfoot who looked too big for his britches and a short, muscular cowboy with pale blue eyes, a thin nose, and a face that would never crack a smile.

"Like to see Midge."

"Who are you?" the tenderfoot asked, a touch snottily.

"Slocum." He paused to light up a cigarillo while the tenderfoot stood stolidly. Slocum stared at him. "How'd you like to tell her I'm here?"

"Go tell her, Terry," said the muscular cowboy. They watched the tenderfoot turn sullenly and saunter toward the house.

"I'm Eddie Corne," the muscular cowboy said. "Think I've heard of you, Slocum."

"Heard what?"

"Good things." Eddie's voice was toneless, and he didn't smile; he never smiled.

"You boys new here?" Slocum asked.

"Yeah, we're new."

"What about Bill and Red?"

Eddie shrugged. "They're herding cattle to the Bar Z ranch toward Phoenix."

Then Midge came out of the ranch house and her face lighted with pleasure. She hurried toward him and planted a kiss on his cheek. Her lovely face glowed. "I've been worried about you, Slocum. I'm so glad you're back in one piece." She stared at him, almost breathless. Then she said, "Oh, this is Eddie and Terry. Mr. Grant sent them to help out. But now tell me what happened."

Slocum nodded; it had been smart not to talk in front of them. He took her arm and walked to the privacy of the chairs near the ranch house. Rosa brought out coffee.

Midge was looking at him. "Slade?"

"Dead," he said.

She bit her lip. Apparently she had wanted revenge, but his death jarred her. "A terrible man. A dangerous gunfighter. I feared for you."

Slocum nodded grimly. His shoulder still ached.

"Steele shoot him?" she asked. "Steele and his boys?"

He shook his head.

She stared, frowned, and her hands went up to fluff her golden hair. "You? That's wonderful. But surely Steele helped?"

"No. He wasn't out to help, Midge."

She scowled, disbelieving. "What do you mean?"

"I can't figure it. Steele had set me up for killing. I was lucky. Got help from a stranger, a man with a rifle."

She stared at him with big eyes, digesting it all. "But why would he do that?"

Slocum smiled wryly. "It's a mystery. Steele turned on me. Had to shoot him."

"So Steele is dead too." Her voice was flat. Finally she asked, "Who was the man with the rifle?"

"Don't know. Another mystery. He saved my hide. Didn't stick around after, and I wanted to thank him."

She looked thoughtful. "All very strange. Someone on our side. Wonder who he is?"

"That's right, Midge. On our side. Important to know who's on your side."

She looked puzzled. "What do you mean?"

"There are guns against us, that's what I mean."

"What guns?"

He leaned forward. "What do you know about Grant?"

Her look of amazement was genuine. It took almost a minute before she spoke. "Are you going to tell me that Mr. Grant is against us?"

Slocum shrugged his shoulders. "I don't know. Somebody is."

"Why, there's no better friend than Mr. Grant. He was always helpful to Tim. And when Tim was killed he offered me help. Money. Men to help on the ranch. He sent Steele to pay Slade off. What about all that, Slocum? Even those two cowboys there, Eddie and Terry, are Grant's men."

Slocum pulled out a cigarillo. It sure sounded persuasive. She couldn't be that far wrong. So had Slade been telling the truth or just playing a game? Amusing himself with a lie with a man he expected to kill within the minute?

What was the answer?

Midge gazed at him thoughtfully, as if she had something on her mind. "Come in the house. I've got some fine apple pie."

They went inside. He ate the pie with coffee, enjoying it while she watched. After finishing, he smacked his lips.

"You liked it," she said.

"Great pie." He looked out the window. The tenderfoot was sitting on the corral fence picking his teeth and watching Eddie examine the ankle of an Appaloosa.

Slocum leaned back in his chair. "What now, Midge? What are you going to do?"

"Do? I'm going to sit around until I have my baby."

Her belly was slightly swelled, but she was still a handsome filly. Slocum had always wondered what had made a woman like her go for Tim Blake, who was not at all a flashy type—solid, true blue, with grit, but real plain-looking.

"Well, Midge, I've got to tell you: Tim didn't get shot just because Slade was drunk."

She gazed at him bleakly. "Why did Slade do it?"

"He did it for fifty dollars."

She stared at him with disbelief. "Slade told you that? That he was paid fifty dollars?"

Slocum nodded. "Just before the draw. He figured he had nothing to worry about, telling me. He expected I'd be dead next minute."

She bit her lip. "Who was it that paid him?"

"He didn't say."

"I don't believe it," she said angrily. "Slade was rotten clear through. Why would anyone pay him to do that? Tim didn't have an enemy in Black Rock."

Slocum picked up his coffee cup. It might not be true. Who would pay Slade to shoot Tim? Lots of mysteries. Why'd Steele turn on him? Why did gunmen shoot at him in Bitter Creek and Black Rock? And who the hell was the stranger with the rifle?

Maybe the stranger had some answers. But where would Slocum find him? After sharpshooting Amos, he had disappeared.

Slocum sighed. Far from feeling easy, now that Slade was dead there seemed to be more to worry about.

That stranger? He'd seen him first in Tully's Deadeye Saloon in Black Rock. Might be a good idea to ride in and hang around. Slocum felt he was still somebody's target. Somebody wanted him dead.

Midge was watching him. "What about you, Slocum, now that Slade's gone?"

"Maybe Slade was just the gun," he said. "Maybe someone else is the killer."

She shook her head. "Who, Slocum?"

He smiled grimly. "Every once in a while a stranger hears my name and takes a potshot at me. There's plenty out there aching for revenge. Kin to the polecats I've done in."

She looked thoughtful. "I've been wondering if it might be safer for you to ride out of Black Rock. For a while. I'd feel better. I'd hate for you to risk your life. I've lost Tim, and nobody's blood is going to bring him back. Maybe things in Black Rock will be quiet now that Slade's gone."

Slocum stood up slowly. "I don't like being a target, Midge. Someone's been trying to pick me off since Bitter Creek. He's not going to stop because I stop. No, Midge. Better if I stick around and try to smoke out what's behind all this. Now I'm going into town."

Outside, as he walked toward his horse, he noted the tenderfoot still picking his teeth. It fitted his idea of what a red-blooded cowboy did. But it took more than that, Slocum thought.

Eddie sauntered toward him, his pink face serious. "Now that Slade's gone, I reckon you aim to ride on?"

Slocum put his hand on the saddle and looked into Eddie's eyes. He didn't seem to care one way or another. "Mister, I've learned this thing—one town's just as bad as another. I'll hang on for a couple of days to see if anything exciting happens."

Eddie nodded solemnly. "You never know in Black Rock. Peace one day, five men dead the next."

Slocum smiled. "Here today, dead tomorrow. That's the territories."

The tenderfoot spoke up with a grin of pride. "We've got more folks in Boot Hill than in the town, Slocum."

Slocum smiled cheerfully as he swung over the saddle. "Reminds me of Tombstone."

Slocum rode into Black Rock at night, when the oil lamps from the houses spilled light on the dirt street. Inside the Deadeye things were bright and brassy. Cowboys drinking and carousing, and the card tables were busy.

At the bar, Tully, a bit astonished, looked at Slocum, as he put down a whiskey bottle and filled a glass.

"Surprised to see me, Tully?"

Tully leaned close to him and spoke in a low voice. "In this town, Slocum, gunfighters have a short life. Now, take Steele, for example. Ain't nobody seen him lately."

Slocum poured a drink and quaffed it. He wiped his mouth. "Maybe he's gone to the big gunfighter roundup in the sky."

Tully glanced quickly at him. "That's how it goes," he said, then went off to another customer.

Slocum took the bottle and glass to an empty table near a card game, sat down, and poured another drink. He soon began to feel easy. He watched the men at the bar for a time, then the players at the table, then wondered if maybe he should ride out to Grant's and tell him that his men got all shot up. Well, there was time enough for that. He drank again, and when a player stood to leave a poker game, he walked over to the table. The players looked at him. "Mind if I join?" he asked.

"Your money's good as anyone's," said one burly man.

He had been playing for half an hour, staying about even, when the doors swung open and Grant came in with three hard, brawny men. He always seemed to have a tough escort. Spotting Slocum playing cards, his face tightened and he strolled to the table, followed by his men.

He stood there, studying Slocum, then smiled. "Glad to see you in one piece, mister."

Slocum stared into the cool gray eyes. "Wasn't easy, considering all the fireworks."

Grant looked serious and waited silently.

Slocum slowly rose to his feet. "Deal me out."

Grant walked to an empty table in the back of the saloon, and Slocum followed. The three riders moved over to the bar, watching with blank, expressionless eyes.

Tully sent a man to Grant with a bottle of his best whiskey and some glasses. Grant poured two shots. He lifted his drink, waiting for Slocum. But Slocum lit a cigarillo.

Grant said, "I'm a bit disappointed in you, Slocum."

Slocum puffed his cigarillo.

Grant went on. "I expected you might ride out to my place and tell me what happened. I had to find out from one of my men that you hit town."

Slocum just smoked.

Then Grant said, "Where's Steele?"

Slocum took the cigarillo from his mouth. "Dead."

Grant was startled. He hadn't expected that. "Steele? What about Lonnie and Amos?"

Slocum nodded. "Them too."

Grant thought about it. He reached slowly into his breast pocket, pulled out a cigar, and lit it. "And Slade, what about him?" His tone seemed anxious. "Did Slade do the killing?"

"Slade's dead too." Slocum's voice was flat.

"That's something, at least. How'd it happen? Big shootout? Was that it? They all went down?"

"No. I got Slade."

"*You* got Slade?" He digested that, glanced at his men standing at the bar, holding drinks, watching, alert. Grant spoke slowly. "So Slade's dead. Well, we finally did our bit for Tim Blake."

Slocum said nothing.

Grant studied Slocum, and a grim smile spread over his face. "You've got a talent for survival, Slocum. I admire that."

"I try," Slocum said. "It's mighty hard, especially when men you trust turn on you."

Grant's jaw hardened. "What's that mean?"

"I mean Steele. He turned a gun on me. He was going to blast me."

Grant scowled. "What happened?" he demanded.

"Some crack rifleman downhill saw it and fired. Saved my hide."

Grant stroked his chin. "Lucky. Who the hell did it?"

"That's what I'd like to know."

Then Grant smiled. "So some gunman saved your hide."

"That's right."

Grant nodded thoughtfully. "I'm sure that Midge Blake was plenty grateful when you told her everything."

Slocum said nothing.

"Are you finished around here, Slocum?

"I don't know."

There was a long pause while Grant did some heavy thinking. "You're a top gun, Slocum. Come join me and my men. I'll pay good money."

"To do what?"

"Keep the peace. Knock off rustlers. Protective work. Like that. We've got some fast guns. You'd like it."

Slocum looked at the gray eyes, flat and expressionless. "Let me think about it."

A slow smile broke over Grant's face. "Be good to have you with us, Slocum. Don't take too long thinking."

Slocum stood up and walked slowly past the bar, where Grant's three henchmen stood watching him. They all had the same blank look, like men who didn't care who they pointed their guns at, once their boss gave the command to kill.

Slocum went out into the night street, where two cowboys were drinking heavily from whiskey bottles. They whooped it up, one throwing his empty bottle into the air and shooting it to pieces. The other, a man with a heavy mustache, seemed particularly fierce. He still held his bottle, and he looked around for amusement. He saw Slocum through fuzzy eyes and yelled to his sidekick, "Here's a cowboy who'll give us a dance." And pointing his gun down, he fired a couple of bullets at Slocum's feet.

The feet didn't move, not an inch. The drunk holding his Colt in one hand, his bottle in the other, looked astonished that the feet hadn't moved, and for the first time his gaze went up to Slocum's face. He saw eyes that were twin slits of icy green.

Slocum's hand slithered to his holster, a dazzling movement as his gun fired twice, the first bullet smashing the Colt, the next exploding the bottle, leaving the drunk holding its broken neck.

There was a moment of silence as the two men suddenly sobered, stared at Slocum. They began to back off slowly, watching him. Then they turned and ran for their horses.

As Slocum watched them, a face appeared at the second story of the saloon. It was Lori, the dance girl. She smiled down at him.

He walked to his horse, mounted up, and rode out of town. The skies were littered with millions of stars. He soon found a sheltered nook, pulled out his bedroll, and lay back, hands behind his head.

For a while he looked at the starry sky, then his

thoughts drifted to Grant. Why would this strange gent want his gun and be willing to pay so well? Because he had rustling problems? That seemed a sound reason.

Though he felt uneasy about Grant, there was nothing to hang it on. If anyone knew Grant well, it would be Midge. She had the best opportunity to know him; he was a neighbor. And Midge described him as a friend, generous, honest, helpful.

Slocum looked at the big stars gleaming brightly in the dark blue sky and felt easier. He wondered if he'd been reading Grant wrong; he tended to be suspicious of big cattlemen, having learned how often they acquired their land through harsh measures.

The serenity of the heavens was soothing, and within minutes sleep came over him.

8

The next morning after breakfast Slocum rode west. A big sun was climbing behind the great silhouettes of stone when he sighted the prints of two unshod horses. He came alert. The prints were fresh and meant Apaches were nearby. Two Apaches moving west, following a parallel trail. Tracking. They had picked up a lone rider, which could mean booty: horses, guns, clothing.

Braves were always on the lookout for single riders.

Taking his rifle, he slipped off the roan and moved in a crouch. His keen ears picked up a soft sound, and, noiselessly, he moved forward. Finally he spotted them: they had their victim on the ground, a cowboy in a dark brown shirt. They had stripped him of his boots, hat, and gun.

Somehow they'd managed to surprise him and were now ready to leave him tied like a roped calf, prey to prowling carnivores. Apaches had harsh ideas of revenge for the white devils who had despoiled their land.

Something about the look of the captured white man caught Slocum's eye, and his mouth tightened. It was none other than the cowboy who had saved his life with the rifle shot that blew Amos apart. He'd also shot two Apaches on the trail to Ledville. Did these two Apaches know, and had they been trailing him?

Slocum inched up, silent as a shadow. One Apache, well muscled, was leaning down to tie the cowboy's legs, but, as Slocum suspected, it was a feint, for he was already aware of an intruder, because with a quick half swing he brought up his rifle to fire. Slocum's rifle barked first, and the Apache jumped, then fell. The other Apache threw a barrage of bullets at Slocum's position, slipping behind the body and using it as a shield. Slocum ducked behind rock cover. To keep the redskin from throwing a bullet at the prone cowboy, Slocum kept firing, forcing him to go for his mustang behind the rocks. Crouched tight against its body, he beat his heels into its flank, and the horse ran a twisting trail north. By the time Slocum came out from behind his rock, the Apache was outside the range of accurate fire.

Slocum moved forward. When he reached the two sprawled bodies, the Apache suddenly came to life, grabbing at his rifle. Slocum tugged it back, firing twice, and the Apache jumped and fell back, two gaping holes in his body.

The cowboy's face was pale. He'd been hit with a tomahawk—a glancing blow on the head—and suffered a small loss of blood. But he was conscious and aware of what had been happening. He gave Slocum a small smile and sat up.

"You seem to spend a lot of time in my neighborhood, mister," Slocum said grimly.

"I suppose so." He put his hand to his head tenderly. "A near miss. They sneaked up on me real good."

"Who the hell are you?" Slocum asked.

He leaned back on his two hands and looked up. "The name is Blake. Charlie Blake. I'm kin to Tim."

"Kin?" There was a moment of silence.

"Yeah, Tim was my half brother. Same father, different mother."

Slocum didn't know much about Tim's family, but once Tim had mentioned kin in Texas. Now Slocum remembered that his first sight of Charlie Blake reminded him of someone. Well, he looked like Tim. Charlie Blake was craggy-faced, sinewy, tall, with light curly hair and blue eyes.

He was wiping blood from his head and spoke slowly. "Tim wrote to me, like he did to you. Told me that John Slocum, his ole sidekick in the war, would be comin' to Black Rock to help. Tim said he had plenty of trouble. They were closing in on him. That's what he said. Wrote me to maybe keep a watch on you."

"He told you that?" Slocum scratched his head. The story seemed odd. Yet Charlie had kept a watch on him. He'd been in the saloon during the fistfight. He'd been on the trail to Black Rock. To Ledville. And when Steele and Amos had him trapped, it was Charlie and his rifle that had saved his hide.

"But why keep a watch on me?"

"He figured those who were out to get him would go after you, too, that's why. Turned out to be that Steele bunch. Then I began to think it might be Grant giving Tim trouble."

"Why Grant?"

Charlie shook his head. "Maybe because Tim wondered about Grant one time—whether he wanted his stream." Charlie smiled grimly. "Grant strikes me as a man who takes no chances. Maybe he knew you were coming."

Slocum thought of Seth, back in Bitter Creek, who had paid Annabelle to set him up. And the gunfighter who'd tried to get a bullet in him during a poker game. Was that all meant to stop him from reaching Black Rock?

If it was Grant, what did Grant have against Tim? Was there something on the Blake land? Tim wouldn't sell, and without Tim, Midge would be easy pickings. So maybe Grant put Slade on Tim.

Could Grant be the joker behind Slade? But why would Slade ride back to Black Rock? Because Grant's ace gunfighter, Steele, had been trailing him. Slade figured that Grant had sent Steele to wipe him out, that he knew too much. And Slade aimed to pay Grant off.

Did all this make sense or was it just a series of incidents with no real connection?

There was no proof of anything.

He wondered why Grant always rode with three gunfighters as bodyguard. And now Grant wanted to hire him as a gun. He looked at Charlie. "Can you ride?"

"I can ride."

"We'll go out to Midge and fix you up there. See what she knows. Either Grant is a square shooter or one tricky dog."

Charlie nodded. He moved painfully.

Slocum glanced at the dead Apache. "Reckon we'd better bury him. We don't want Apache revenge for Apache dead."

After they buried him, they rode toward the Blake ranch. On the trail, Slocum spotted a herd of white-tailed deer and some game birds that flew straight up as they approached. He picked off a bird, and they stopped on a grassy knoll to fry its meat. After eating, they drank coffee with a splash of whiskey, and Slocum looked at the mountains in the distance, glinting in the bright sun.

A full stomach and hot coffee made him glow, and he realized how much he loved the West, with its great mountains, its vast space, and the sense of freedom it gave a man's spirit.

As Charlie lit a cigar, Slocum glanced at his craggy face and marveled at his strong likeness to Tim Blake. They had the same father, he had said. Slocum wondered if he had known Midge in the early days.

"I reckon you knew Midge as a young filly," Slocum said.

Charlie nodded and began to laugh as memories tumbled into his mind. "Yeah, I knew her as a freckled-face brat, and as a tomboy. But you never saw such a change when she started to grow up. She just blossomed out, all pink and roses. The town lads went wild. She loved that, being the cutest filly in town. But she was out to lasso Tim. He was the best of the lads—the smartest and bravest. No dare he wouldn't take."

Slocum remembered Tim Blake holding a rifle, standing alongside him, firing. He wouldn't crouch because it didn't seem brave.

Charlie sipped his coffee as he recalled the past. "The gals set their bonnets for him, but Midge nailed him down. She had to beat them all. Says to him one day, 'Tim Blake, you and me are goin' to get hitched, whether the war happens or not.' They married before the war, and were going strong. But when he came back, things were different. Started to go sour. Maybe it was the war, I don't know. When he wrote me that she'd gotten pregnant, I figured it would fix it between them." Charlie shook his head.

Slocum thought of Midge, a good-looking woman. She seemed to know what was happening. He liked her, but she wasn't easy to figure. "What do you think about Midge?" he asked.

Charlie took off his flat hat that he wore with its front pushed back. He looked at it deliberately. "Tell you the truth, Slocum, I never cared that much about her." He smiled grimly. "Maybe because she didn't care much about me."

Slocum rubbed his chin thoughtfully. "A nice-looking woman. She's got a kid coming. Women get edgy in that time, I reckon."

"Maybe that's it," Charlie said, snuffing out his cigar.

"So, how're you feeling now?"

"The head aches a bit, but it'll pass."

Slocum smiled. "Lucky he didn't get a full hit. Would of busted your brains."

Charlie grinned. "Wouldn't make much difference. They're busted plenty now."

The both smiled, finished their coffee, then started for their horses.

The sun glowed yellow in the blue sky and a west wind gently blew the grasses as they rode toward the Blake ranch.

Charlie was silent and seemed almost sullen. Something bothered him, but Slocum was too preoccupied with his own thoughts to worry about it. When they reached the hilltop and could look down on the ranch, they could see Eddie and Terry in the corral, branding a roped calf. Midge was watching as she leaned on the fence. They all turned to look at Slocum and Charlie as they rode toward the ranch house.

Midge came to meet them, staring at Charlie as they swung off their horses. "Charlie Blake," she said with surprise. "You here? Imagine that." She stared at the side of his head. "Now, what hit you?"

He put his hand to his head. "Couple of Apaches. Would've got my scalp but for Slocum."

She flashed Slocum a look. "Can't beat *him*." She turned to Charlie. "Can I do anything? Put a fresh bandage on that."

"I'll be all right, Midge. Just a stiff drink."

She kept staring in wonder. "I must confess you surprised me, Charlie. Why didn't you let me know you were comin'?" She bit her lip. "Reckon you heard about Tim."

"I heard." Charlie's face was grim. "And you pregnant."

Her lips were tight and her blue eyes gleamed. "Terrible." She turned to Slocum and managed a smile. "Come into the house. I've got good whiskey. Let me give you boys a home-cooked meal. Would you like that?"

"We'd like that," Slocum said.

They went into the house and got washed up, and it didn't take too long before they were sitting in the comfortable dining room. There was plenty of good beef stew, and dishes of corn, okra, and beans. The men ate with gusto, and they all had apple pie and coffee for dessert.

Slocum felt the warmth of a home, but one where the man of the house was missing. Charlie felt it too, for his mood was heavy. There was an edge about Midge.

After they had finished the pie, they were silent. Midge refilled their coffee cups, then said, "There's something on your mind, Charlie. What is it?"

Charlie rubbed his lips nervously. "Yeah, I been wondering, Midge. I'd like you to think about the ranch. Is there something on it that's, well, valuable?"

She looked puzzled. "Why, Charlie, we've got a fine stream, good grass, cattle—they're all valuable."

"What about that stream? Someone want it real bad?" Slocum asked.

She looked thoughtful. "Grant's cattle use it. But he never made an offer for it."

"Anything else, Midge?" Charlie said, leaning forward. "Think. Something hidden on it? Like gold?"

She laughed "You're dreaming Charlie. Nothing like that on our land."

Slocum shrugged. "Won't be the first time gold's been buried on land. Apache gold. Gang gold."

She was staring at him. "Are you going to hit again on Mr. Grant?"

Charlie grimaced. "I've gotta tell you, Midge, it could be that Grant has his eye on your land for some reason—and it's got to profit him. We think he might be behind the things happening here."

Her eyes opened in astonishment, then blazed with

anger. But she didn't speak until she got herself under control. "What things? I've told Slocum, and I'll tell you honestly that I have the highest regard for Mr. Grant. He's four-square and straight."

Charlie looked away, embarrassed for a moment, then looked directly at her. "Midge, I've gotta tell you. Tim wrote to me. Told me that they were closin' in on him."

She looked startled. "He wrote that? Who was closing in?" Her voice was harsh.

"He didn't say."

"Where's that letter?"

Charlie shook his head. "I don't have it."

She breathed deeply. "I'm not going to doubt you, Charlie Blake, but I can't believe Tim had Grant in mind. Mr. Grant wouldn't do anything bad. He's always been helpful and generous to us."

Charlie's voice was cool. "But what does 'closing in' mean?"

Slocum said, "A man would say that if he felt himself in danger."

"What danger?" she demanded.

"Plenty danger. Because Tim's not here anymore," Slocum said.

She looked depressed, then thought about it. "Gunmen kept pushing him. I begged him not to go to the Deadeye Saloon."

Slocum toyed with his fork. "So somebody wanted Tim out. Why?"

She frowned. "I don't know. There are crazy gunmen willing to shoot anyone, once their blood gets hot."

"It's more than that," Slocum said. He told her of his suspicions about Slade and Steele.

She stared at him. "So you're hitting on Grant again. I can't imagine that he'd want to hurt Tim. Or me. You've got him all wrong."

Slocum lit a cigarillo thoughtfully. Could he be wrong about Grant? Or was he such a good actor that he had her completely bamboozled?

"Why would Grant want to hurt Tim?" she demanded. "What could he hope to get? We don't have buried gold. All right, we've got a stream. But he wouldn't have Tim killed for water he was getting free." She stared at him. "Don't you see how wrong you are? Somehow you started with the idea that Mr. Grant was behind it all, then you fitted every incident in that picture. No, you're both wrong about Mr. Grant."

Slocum looked at Charlie. There was sense to her argument. She could be right. He did tend to believe the worst of big ranchmen, convinced they became big by using unscrupulous ways.

Charlie looked halfway persuaded.

Midge considered them. "If you came to know him, you'd admire him. He's strong and generous. Yes, he goes after what he wants, but what red-blooded man doesn't?"

She lifted the coffee cup to her lips. "I feel you've done your job. Slade is gone. Tim is avenged. And you're not badly hurt. It could have been worse. I want nothing more to happen to you. That's why I say this. You could just ride on, Slocum. Get away from Black Rock and its bloody ways. At least for a time."

Slocum smiled. She worried about him like a cow over its calf. Didn't want him getting hurt. "Reckon I can take care of myself, Midge. But you may be right. Slade's been paid off. No point hanging on in Black

Rock. Been aimin' to ride to Tombstone, anyway. Reckon I'll head out tomorrow." He turned to Charlie Blake. "What about you?"

Charlie looked moody, then sighed. "Reckon it's all right. I just hope you're gonna have peace and quiet around you, Midge." He glanced at her swelled stomach. "Seeing what's ahead for you, it'll be nice to have some easy days."

That night Slocum and Charlie Blake rode out of the ranch, heading for Tombstone. It was a starry night, and the moon laid a silver blanket over the land and the soaring mountains in the distance. After riding for a while, they broke for camp, made a fire, and ate.

During the ride, Charlie had been mostly silent and preoccupied, but after eating and drinking coffee he seemed more inclined to talk. He lit a cheroot. "Even before we met, Slocum, I figured I knew you. Tim would bust my ear taking about the war."

Slocum looked at him. Charlie's craggy face gleamed in the light of the fire. He wore a blue shirt under his gray vest, and a black kerchief around his neck. "Some soldiers," Slocum said, "when they come out of the war, never top talking about it. Others never *start* talking."

Charlie's craggy face crinkled about his blue eyes. "Tim said you were the sharpest rifle eye he'd ever seen. Kept pickin' off the Union brass."

Slocum looked solemn. Some of his cronies liked to talk about the war. And the war sounded romantic to those who weren't there, but it was mean and terrible to those who were. When it came to his mind, he heard the groans of dying men and saw the torn bodies and bloody corpses.

As a soldier, he had been ordered to kill, but he expected to be finished with guns afterward. Yet when he got back to his plantation in Georgia, he was confronted by a carpetbagger judge who claimed a right to his land. His land, that for generations had belonged to the Slocums. His rage had been fierce and his gun quick. The carpetbagger's claim to the Slocum plantation went six feet deep.

After that, he went on the run. His drifting brought him west to the territories, where the gun was the law and survival depended on the speed of your draw. Yes, he'd been able to survive, but he showed the scars of battle.

Charlie was smiling. "Tim told me once that the luckiest thing that ever happened to him was fighting alongside you."

"Why'd he say that?"

"Reckon that's where he felt safe."

Slocum's mouth was tight. "Not safe enough. He was next to me when he caught a bullet in the groin. Put him in the hospital for three months."

Charlie looked thoughtful. "Yeah, that hurt him." He snuffed his cheroot. "I just wonder sometimes."

Slocum leaned forward a bit. "Wonder what?"

"About them. Together. I told you, things between them changed a bit afterward." He frowned.

Slocum seemed not to be listening but was just looking up at the stars. They were big and bright in the sky. "Just keep talking and bring your body down, like you're reaching for a coffee cup," he said, smiling. "We've got a sneaky coyote behind you in the bushes. I'll take care of him when he makes his next move. But there's another hombre, who I can't locate."

Charlie took a deep breath, and his body slowly went lower. Slocum's hand flashed to his holster and came up spitting a bullet. A man yelped with pain. Slocum threw himself to the ground just as gunfire from the rocks on his right lit the dark. The bullets whistled past his ear. As Slocum rolled, he fired in its direction. There was a scuttling of rocks and the dim sound of running boots.

"He's out there," Slocum whispered.

Charlie, flat on his belly behind the big rock, was breathing hard. He had his gun in hand but couldn't see anything to shoot. "Goddamn, Slocum, how long did you know they were out there?"

"Just picked it up. They must have followed our trail soon after we left the Blake place."

"Who the hell is it?"

"The ranch hands at Midge's place. Eddie and Terry."

"Why the hell were they trailing us?"

"Let's find out."

They crawled forward to a cluster of dry, harsh shrubs and found Terry lying in a pool of blood. He'd been hit in the neck, and the blood gushed out. He wasn't dead, but near enough. Nothing they could get from him.

The second barrage of shots had come from a bunch of raw splintered rocks to the right; crouched down, they moved cautiously toward it. When they finally got there, they found only the smears of booted prints.

The prints led them to the heavy bushes, where

Eddie had tethered his horse. He was gone, though.

Charlie scratched his head. "Why'd they do this, you reckon?"

There was a moment of silence. "They're Grant's men," Slocum said. "That's why."

Charlie's face twisted as he worked on that. "But we were leaving Black Rock. Why should Grant try this?"

Slocum thought about it. "Maybe Grant didn't know we were planning to leave. How could he know? He told these coyotes to nail us and they tried it."

"Why is Grant so hellfire set on wiping us out? What have we done to him?"

Slocum grinned fiendishly. "Nothing. And that's what's eating my tail."

"You figure the other polecat, Eddie, might know?"

Slocum shook his head. "I doubt it. Grant knows. He's damned set on getting me dead. Set on it for a long time—all the way back to Bitter Creek. He's gotta have some hellish reason. I can't imagine that reason, but I'll find out if it's the last thing I do."

"What about Eddie? Do we go after him?"

"Pure waste of time. He won't know anything. Grant's the man. And it's hard to nail him. Can't go to his ranch—too many guns. We've got to figure another way."

Charlie looked at Slocum's lean, hard-boned, leather-brown face, creased with concentration.

Finally Slocum said, "How'd you like to get back to the Blake ranch? Help Midge with the chores. After all, she's lost two ranch hands. Eddie won't show. Hang on and see what you can find out. Grant seems to visit Midge."

Charlie nodded. "I'll do it."

Slocum fingered his chin. "Looks like Grant is deep in this game. Probably he's the man behind Slade's gun."

"Sounds right to me." Charlie shut his eyes, concentrating, trying to remember something. "You know," he said finally, "Slade came out of Tombstone. I wonder if you'd learn something if you moseyed down to Tombstone and hung around the saloon. It's only a three-hour ride, and it might be worth it. What do you think, Slocum?"

"Not a bad idea. Grant might think I've gone and let his guard down. And you could learn something too."

They looked at each other and smiled.

"The main thing," Slocum said, "is not to get into a mixup at the Deadeye. Not till I get back. You hear me?"

"I hear you."

"I'll go for Tombstone," Slocum said.

9

John Grant came out of his big white ranch house, stood in the doorway, and looked around at his land. Under the huge yellow sun, it seemed to stretch far as he could see. The sight of great herds of cattle gratified him. There was no counting his stock. All he knew was that he was known as the biggest cattle king this side of Arizona, and he had no intention of losing that title.

He stared east toward the Blake ranch and thought about their stream. A good stream, but he didn't need it. Not yet. Midge let his stock use the stream, so why buy it? But if there came a time when he might need water, he'd know how to get it.

Rudabaugh, his foreman, came riding up and swung off his Appaloosa. "Got a piece of bad news, Mr. Grant."

Grant scowled. He didn't like bad news this early. "What is it?"

"Terry's dead."

Grant thought of the brash young gunman that he'd sent over to Midge. "How'd it happen?" His voice was curt.

"He and Eddie were trailing Slocum and Blake like you wanted. When they tried to bushwhack them, Terry got picked off. Happened south of Rust Hills."

Grant's gray eyes were glacial. "What about Eddie?"

"He's here. Told me they followed your instructions. Tried to hit them when they camped."

"Rust Hills? What the hell were they doin' that far north?"

"Ridin' to Tombstone, I reckon."

"They were leavin' town?"

"Looks like it."

"So why'd those two jugheads try to hit them? Why didn't they just let them ride? I'd like them dead sure, but if they ride out, that might be good too."

Rudabaugh shrugged. "You told the boys to shoot the hell outa them. They tried."

Grant's face reddened with anger. "Damn jugheads. Now Slocum's goin' to come back. It's gotta be clear to him who's shooting at him."

Rudabaugh looked thoughtful. Grant had never told him why he wanted Slocum and Charlie Blake dead, and he had never asked. He had worked for Grant a long time, but Grant was a hard man with a tight mouth. He didn't confide. He gave orders and expected them to be carried out. He could be ruthless. He paid good money and expected total loyalty. He was rich, had a huge ranch, and there were plenty of rustlers and drifters who

liked to pilfer a piece of it. Grant ordered quick lynch-
ings for those caught. Yet he could be generous, as he
was to Midge Blake, who had the neighboring ranch.

"I've always been curious, boss. What do you have
against those two polecats?"

Grant turned his hard gray eyes on him. "That's my
business, Rudabaugh. Your business is to do what I want,"
he said and pulled down the brim of his big Stetson.

Rudabaugh's lips tightened. That was it, you
couldn't get close to this bastard. "I'm sorry, Mr. Grant.
I just thought Midge Blake might be a bit grieved to lose
her kin. And you've got a soft spot for her."

Grant's jaw hardened. "You're thinkin' too much,
mister. Let me do that." He looked thoughtfully out at
his great herds. "I've got a great stock out there and a
good rep in the territory. I cherish all that and I don't
want to spoil it. Keep that in mind, Rudabaugh."

He pulled a cigar from his waist pocket and lit it,
thinking all the time. Then he cleared his throat. "Now
about Slocum and Blake. They gotta go down. But we
don't bushwack them; it hasn't worked, they're too
smart. No more backstabbin'. We'll get them in a
straight draw, head-on. Now, here's what I want. You
ride to Tombstone, get hold of Kid Cassidy or Doc Holliday, if he's not coughin' too much. Tell 'em I've got a
job. Top money." He grinned evilly. "We're goin' to put
the fastest gun against these blasted polecats. I won't
rest easy till then. Specially, I don't want those polecats
hangin' too long around the Blake ranch. Are we clear
about that, Rudabaugh?"

Rudabaugh nodded. There it was. The whole mystery seemed to circle the Blake ranch. Something there
threw a hook into Grant. Did he want the land, to ex-

pand his place? The stream? But why worry about Slocum and Blake? Where they there to stop him? Still, Grant couldn't push the pregnant widow, Midge Blake, off the land without getting a bad rap from the town. And he liked having a good reputation. Rudabaugh shrugged. Well, it was no skin off his back. He'd do what Grant wanted. He was paid plenty for his loyalty.

Grant was staring at him. "Whatcha dreamin' about, Rudabaugh? You got a lot to do."

"I'm gone to Tombstone," Rudabaugh said, walking to his horse.

Grant watched him as he swung over his saddle and started to ride. He watched until the foreman became a small speck on the horizon, but his thoughts, all that time, were on Slocum. And suddenly Grant became aware that his body was tight with fear and hate.

Midge Blake, her golden hair glowing in the sun, her violet eyes shining with pleasure, rode her newly broken mare around the corral. The mare's disposition was naturally gentle, she moved with an easy gait, and if there was one thing Midge needed now, it was a gentle ride. In truth, she was thinking, it wouldn't be long before her riding would be restricted to the buggy.

She was carrying a precious burden—a child. The very thought sent a surge of joy through her. Giving birth to a child had been the focus of her life. It had always been like that for her, even as a young girl. The rhythms of nature flowed strongly in her, and she believed she could only find true fulfillment by giving birth. How she'd come to this belief, she suspected, went back to her childhood, when her neighbor had given birth to a male baby. She'd been seven and from

time to time was permitted to take care of it. Like a
living doll, that baby. That had been the high point of
her childhood memories. To take charge of that wonderful creature, all pink and shiny, with big blue eyes,
looking with wonder out at the big world. Yes, she
wanted one of her own, yearned for it, her breasts
yearned to suckle a baby. And now, within months she
would have her own child.

Then she saw the rider and her eyes widened. Charlie
Blake. Her mind worked frantically on the meaning. He
was supposed to be riding out toward Tombstone, so
why had he come back? And alone. Where was Slocum? Strange things were happening. Eddie and Terry
had gone off without a single word to her. It had to be
guns, it was always guns, she thought. Guns had been
part of her life with Tim Blake. Living on the ranch in
the early days, she had come to know Apaches, drifters,
derelicts, rustlers, wandering thieves.

But when John Grant took over the big tract of land
next to them, things steadied down. Grant's men kept
out the intruders. Tim said, in the early days, that the
day Grant came to Black Rock was solid gold. A
shadow crossed her mind when she thought of Tim. A
gun had taken him, too. But there was no point in remembering the past. She lived in a new and different
world now.

But what was she to make of Charlie, who had come
onto the ranch?

She reined the mare, swung off her, patted her warm
neck, then walked out of the corral to meet him. He was
smiling. That was reassuring. She never knew how to
handle Charlie. He was so different from Tim, his half
brother, and yet he did have the Blake streak, the same

father. Even looked like him in certain lights, the craggy face, curly hair, light blue eyes. Still, she had never warmed up to Charlie. There was an edge between them. But she tried never to show it, for Tim's sake.

"Weren't you heading for Tombstone?" she asked.

"We were," he said, "but we changed our minds."

Her violet eyes were cool. "What changed it?"

He decided not to tell her about the sneak attack of Eddie and Terry. There'd be time for that. "Slocum went on to Tombstone for business. I thought, if it was all right with you, I'd stay here for maybe a few days, then head on to Phoenix."

He looked around. "You seem short of working men, Midge. While I'm here, I might pitch in and earn my keep. Looks like there'll be plenty of chores to do."

She gazed at him, a bit conflicted. She wasn't crazy about his spending time on the ranch. Still, it was a nice offer. Especially since Terry and Eddie had vanished. She could use help. "Well, Charlie, if you feel you want to pitch in, I'd appreciate it. There's plenty of work. Tim used to manage everything. I'm adrift and can use all the help I can get."

"Count on me," he said cheerfully.

"What about Slocum? Will he be coming back?"

"I hope so." He scowled. "Trouble is, wherever he goes, somebody's taking a shot at him. He leads a dangerous life."

Her eyebrows raised. "Why are they shooting at him?"

Charlie opened his hands in wonder. "It's a mystery, Midge."

"Well," she said, "I hope things get quiet. At this time, I need all the quiet I can get."

He looked at her slightly swelled belly and nodded, and when his gaze returned to her face, he was startled at her expression. She was staring at something.

He turned. Riders were coming toward them, three bulky horsemen, and in front of them rode Grant.

Before they reached the ranch, Grant turned and threw an order at his men. At the ranch, Grant swung down off his saddle and came to meet Midge and Charlie. The three men rode past Charlie, looking at him blankly, and dismounted when they reached the corral.

Grant looked fixedly at Charlie with gray expressionless eyes, then turned to Midge. "Howdy, Miss Midge. Thought I'd stop over and see if things are all right. No ranch trouble?" He glanced at the mare. "I wonder if it's wise for you to be ridin' a horse? A mite dangerous, isn't it?" His voice was courteous and his attitude friendly, which startled Charlie. He knew this powerful rancher to be arrogant and bullish. Grant seemed to belong to that school of western men who treated women with high courtesy, especially pregnant ladies. Such ladies meant the future of the West.

"Why, Mr. Grant. This horse is the gentlest creature on four legs. Wouldn't dream of giving me trouble." She stroked the horse's neck.

"She better not," he said humorously. "How are things here? Anything you need, anything I can do?"

Charlie heard kindness in his tone, which bewildered him. This was not the Grant he'd heard about—a hard and ruthless landowner, quick to string up a rustler or shoot down a renegade Apache.

As if he sensed Charlie's thoughts, Grant turned.

"This, I reckon, is Tim's brother Charlie. Got the Blake look."

"That's right," she said. "Charlie is kin. Half brother to Tim."

Grant looked sorrowful. "I can't tell you, Charlie Blake, how bad I feel about Tim. The way he went down. Slade did it. Slade—one mean killer. A few drinks and he was ready to kill. I sent my boys after him, you know. Well, there's no more Slade to worry about."

Charlie nodded. No Slade to worry about because of Slocum, not because of Grant's men, who had also been gunned down.

Grant stared at him as if reading his thoughts. His smile was almost wicked. "But that's past history."

Midge, aware of the undercurrent of emotions, then said, "Charlie is going to stick around the ranch for a couple of days, Mr. Grant, to help out."

There was a tense moment, but Grant bit the bullet. "What about Eddie and Terry?"

"They're gone," she said. "Haven't seen them."

Grant looked at Charlie expectantly.

Charlie spoke slowly. "Slocum and me were out near Rust Hills when a couple of skunks threw bullets at us. We nailed one. Who do you suppose it was?"

"No idea." Grant's eyes were stony.

"It was Terry. Cowboy who used to work here. One of your men, I heard. Coulda knocked me over with a feather."

Grant stared hard at Charlie. "He turned rotten, did he? Came to me outa Fort Worth with a good word on him. But you can never tell. A man will smile at you and pull a gun. That's the way of the world."

"The other skunk mighta been Eddie," Charlie added, a touch of malice in his voice.

Grant's jaw was tight. "If Eddie was in this, he's a gone goose. One thing I can't stand is a turncoat." There was a long silence, then Grant paused to light a cigar. "So . . . where's Slocum?"

"Slocum? He's gone to Tombstone."

Grant looked startled. "Why'd he go there?"

Charlie shrugged. "Got business there, he said."

Grant studied him, then puffed at his cigar. "Well, that's that." He turned to Midge. "Tell me, Miss Midge, if I can help you in any way. It's a good thing that you've got Charlie staying here." He jerked his thumb toward his men, lolling at the corral. "You might need more men. If so, I'll be glad to leave a couple."

Charlie's teeth clenched while he waited for Midge to speak. She glanced at him, then smiled. "No thanks, Mr. Grant. Things are fine."

Grant threw a last glance at Charlie, and he felt the iron.

They watched Grant ride off. As his men, following close behind, passed Charlie, they stared at him. This time the menace in their faces was clear.

Midge turned to him with a gleam of triumph in her eyes. "There, that was Grant. A gentleman. As I told you and Slocum."

"He seems okay." Charlie was thoughtful. A man can say something but think something different. How could you know?

She was smiling, as if Grant was now certified clean. "You figured he had a greedy eye on this ranch. But he doesn't. I told you. He doesn't need the stream and doesn't need the land."

"Looks like it."

"*Looks* like it. You're a hard head, Charlie. What do you need to convince you?" Her glance at him was shrewd, as if she was trying to dig something out of his head.

He cleared his throat. "It's all about Terry and Eddie. Why'd they come after us? How do you explain it?"

Her face grew hard. "I don't explain it. If a dog turns vicious, you don't explain it, you shoot it."

Charlie was astonished by her intensity. She probably hated their guts, he thought, for turning on her guests.

Still, these two men had come to her ranch with Grant's blessing. Didn't that make him responsible? Charlie took his hat off and wiped his brow. Well, it sounded like Grant intended to make Eddie pay. If he did that, it might straighten things out a bit. He'd discuss it with Slocum when he came back from Tombstone. He thought of how Grant's men had looked at him—not friendly, to say the least.

Then he wondered how Slocum was doing in Tombstone.

10

It was sundown in Tombstone. Golden light glinted off the house windows on Main Street. Slocum moved the roan down the street, glancing from side to side. Some men drifted along the walks, while others loafed on the porches. A couple of buxom women, arm in arm, laughing at some private joke, came out of the big saloon. As they headed up the street, they noted the powerful, lean rider on the roan and smiled boldly at him. Their voluptuous bodies hit him hard, and he realized how much he craved a woman. He was here in Tombstone to get the lowdown on Slade, but he might mix business with pleasure. He rode to the hitch rack, swung out of the saddle, and looped the reins around the crossbar. He glanced over the huddled shacks at the towering peaks of the mountains catching the sun—they looked like golden spears aimed at heaven.

He stepped up to the porch of the Alhambra Saloon, where a grizzled mule skinner, sitting with his chair perched against the wall, stared at him curiously through pale, washed-out blue eyes.

"Howdy, old-timer." Slocum enjoyed the sight of such men, aware that those tired eyes had probably looked upon the bloodiest times of the early West.

"Howdy, pardner." The old-timer nodded and showed a wondrous grin of gaps and yellow teeth.

Slocum paused and turned to look at the flame-colored sky. "Nice time of day."

"Seen thousands of them," the old-timer said. "Just makes me thirsty."

Slocum smiled. "Come on in and I'll buy you a drink."

The ancient one shook his head. "Thanks. Some other time. I'll jest set here and watch the sun go down."

Slocum pushed open the batwing doors, feeling a bit low because all that seemed to be left for this old-timer was watching sunsets. There were about eight men at the bar, three tables for poker, and several women in short, purple taffeta dresses that showed plenty of flesh loafed about.

The barkeep, whom someone called Barney, came over.

"Whiskey," Slocum said.

Barney who had a red face and a bald head, filled the shot glass, waited for Slocum to toss it off, then refilled it. "Four bits," he said.

There was a mirror behind the bottles on the wall, and Slocum could see the reflection of the men at the bar. A motley crew. Then he looked at the women and was struck particularly by one. She had a pretty face and a womanly body, with sensual curves. She was sitting with a lean, sinewy cowboy who got up, and walked over to a bearded man at another table. They began to talk and seemed to get all wrapped up in their discussion. What astonished Slocum was that nobody wanted to take up the slack with the girl. Men looked at her, but nobody approached.

Slocum spoke to the barkeep. "Give me a bottle." He took it and went over to the girl's table. The sinewy cowboy had noticed, but he went on talking. The girl looked up.

"Mind if I sit down?"

She smiled. "If you're sure you want to."

"That's why I'm here." He poured a drink into her empty glass and one for himself. "What's your name?"

"Marylou."

She had a lovely face, round arms, full breasts. She didn't seem to be the usual saloon girl and showed no eagerness to connect. He wondered why.

"Who was the cowboy sitting with you?"

Her smile was mysterious. "Don't you know?"

"No, I don't."

"Kid Cassidy."

Slocum was a bit jarred. Kid Cassidy was a notorious gunfighter, with a lightning gun, they said. No wonder they didn't bother Marylou. But what the hell, she was a saloon girl.

"Are you two teamed?"

She shrugged. "I belong to nobody."

"In that case," he said, "why don't we go someplace more private."

Her dark eyes studied the green eyed man. "Sure you want to?"

"I want to."

"Follow me." She stood up and glanced over at Kid Cassidy. He looked startled, stared at her, then at Slocum, who ignored him. She went up the stairs and Slocum followed, watching the movement of her buttocks, which to him was pure poetry.

In the room, she undid her dress and stepped out of it. She wore nothing underneath. Her body was pink and beautiful, her breasts well shaped, her stomach flat, and her hips wide.

"Well, Marylou, you're a piece of pastry." He dropped his clothes, and his flesh showed his excitement.

"You look like a hunk of pleasure too," she said, smiling. She walked to the door and turned the key to lock it. "Wouldn't want an interruption."

"No. I'd like to concentrate."

His hands went over and over her body, her breasts, her nipples. He toyed with them, stroked her belly. His finger went to the moist crested apex between her thighs. She sighed with pleasure and looked up at him, fire burning in her eyes. She reached over for his cock, stooped to caress it, then did some marvelous things with it. His body tingled; he ached with tension. He pulled her to the bed, where she spread her thighs. He went into her, pinning her against the bed, and her body twisted wildly under him. She flung her arms around his waist, and her hips heaved against him, meeting his thrusts. They moved in rhythm, and her grip around him became fierce as he kept up his moves. Then, as his tension increased, his thrusts became almost violent, and he held her hips tight. His climax was intense, over-powering.

She twisted fiercely, groaned, and groaned again.

They lay there, breathing hard. Then, as they simmered down, she looked up at him, her eyes glowing. "What's your name?"

"Slocum. John Slocum."

"That was very nice, John Slocum. You sure know how to make a woman happy."

He grinned. "You're not so bad."

After they dressed, he put extra money on the bureau.

She put it under her stocking. Her lovely face now looked somber. "I should warn you to be careful. Kid Cassidy is unpredictable. He may do nothing or he may try to pick a fight." She cleared her throat. "Don't fight, I beg you."

"Does he own you?"

"Nobody does. But some men get peculiar ideas after they have a woman." She arranged her hair. "I didn't know you'd be so nice. So be careful, won't you?"

He smiled. "I'm always careful."

Though Slocum came down the stairs casually, his body was alert, and his eyes swept the saloon. Something was different—maybe the noise level; before going up the stairs, he had heard the sound of jovial men drinking, but now they seemed quiet. He had been in setups like this before; it was like the tension of a crowd about to see someone thrown to the lions.

Be careful of Kid Cassidy, Marylou had said.

Funny thing, the Kid still sat at the same table. He looked calm, his legs stretched out, and to Slocum he seemed dreamy. But even in that posture, you could sense the hidden force of his sinewy, muscled body. As Slocum sauntered to the bar, he felt the furtive eyes of watching men.

The barkeep came over, his face impassive, and filled a shot glass.

"What's the matter?" Slocum asked. "Somebody throw a wet blanket on the party?"

A small smile twisted Barney's lips. His voice was low. "Well, you got balls, mister." He threw a nervous glance in the direction of the Kid. "So far, so good. If we get past the next few minutes, maybe we all won't have to duck. And my mirror won't get broke."

As Slocum calmly quaffed his drink, he looked at the mirror. Kid Cassidy stood and lazily stretched. The saloon went silent and watched him stroll just behind Slocum.

"Did you just blow into town, mister?" The voice was strong, silky with an iron edge.

Slocum turned. The Kid had surprising good looks. His features were put together nicely—a fine, straight nose, a well-molded jaw, and a strong neck. Slocum was astonished by his slate blue eyes with their wild, comic glint.

"Yeah," Slocum said, friendly. "Just blew into town."

"A good town, Tombstone," the Kid drawled.

Slocum smiled grimly. "Not bad. A good town for dying."

That startled the Kid, and his eyes moved approvingly over Slocum. Clearly, he liked a gutsy hombre. "They call it Tombstone because they put up stones in memory of desperate cowboys."

"Desperate cowboys?" Slocum repeated, liking the sound of it.

"I call a cowboy desperate," the Kid drawled, "if he puts a claim on another man's filly."

There was a dead silence as Slocum eyed him coolly. Then the Kid smiled, as if he liked Slocum and had decided against a ruckus. "Reckon, mister, you musta come in here when I wasn't sittin' with Marylou." He spoke as if to himself, as of he didn't want to have to pull his gun on Slocum.

Slocum smiled slowly. "I asked the girl if she was spoken for, and she said she was running free."

The Kid's eyes glazed, but then his feeling for humor returned. "She was just funnin', friend. She knows I'm not happy when she runs free. A wild filly." He paused. "And like any wild filly, I s'pose, she should be tamed."

Slocum suddenly became aware that the noise level in the saloon had gone up, that there'd be no showdown on account of the Kid's jealousy. Showdowns because of Marylou must have happened before, and the men had been hoping it would happen again.

The Kid smiled. "You look like a man who's seen plenty. What do you think is the best way to tame a wild filly?"

Slocum considered it. "A real good filly can't be broke. And sometimes a broken filly is worthless."

The Kid frowned with the effort of thinking of what Slocum meant. Then his mouth stretched in a broad grin. "Dammit, that's true. Nothin' I hate more than a spineless creature of any kind."

His blue eyes were brimming with humor. He might be a killer, but he sure knew how to laugh. He was about to turn away when Slocum said, "Say, Kid, ever meet a man called Slade?"

"Jim Slade?"

"That's the one," Slocum said.

The Kid's blue eyes squinted as he remembered Slade. "I know him. Ole Slade. A hot pistol. A sly dog. Pulls a fast gun."

"Can I buy you a drink, Kid?"

Barney was hovering. The Kid nodded, and the barkeep quickly poured a whiskey. The Kid lifted the glass and emptied it.

"Sure would appreciate it if you'd tell me about Slade," Slocum said.

"Like what?"

"Like was he a gun for hire?"

The Kid's blue eyes chilled. "Are you a lawman?"

Slocum smiled. "No. Not a lawman."

The Kid looked at his empty glass and Barney refilled it. He tossed it, thought a moment, then decided to talk. As if he didn't care much about Slade. "Slade was a gun for hire. Willin' to do dirty jobs, if the money was right. Rudabaugh hired him to kill a man in Black Rock. That's the last I seen of Slade. Reckon he'll turn up here if he's still breathin'." He grinned brightly and his tone was mocking. "Tombstone is home base for lowdown desperadoes."

But Slade's not breathin', Slocum thought. So Rudabaugh hired him. Grant's foreman. That made the connection to Grant clear enough. His jaw hardened. Just as he suspected, Grant was in this up to his neck.

Slade was looking at him. "What brought you to Tombstone, mister? Was it Slade?"

Slocum nodded.

The Kid looked carefully at Slocum, at his hands, his gun, measuring him. A curious grin twisted his lips. "Wouldn't surprise me if Slade's gun hand ain't workin' too good." He looked at Slocum, expecting an answer.

Slocum sighed. "Yeah. It stopped working."

The Kid's face was impassive. "I respect the hand that outdrew Slade." His eyes met Slocum's briefly, then he smiled, glanced over at Marylou, sitting by herself, watching them. He made a half turn. "Been nice talkin' to you, mister. Goin' to talk to this free-running filly. But do me a favor. Stay clear of Marylou. For a time." He smiled gently. "You don't want to spoil my rep in this town."

Slocum watched him saunter back to Marylou's table. Nobody dared look at the Kid, because he moved like a coiled spring, as if waiting for a grin of disrespect.

But it never happened.

Slocum stood at the bar, wondering, what next? He had found what he wanted, so why stay in Tombstone? But it was late, and there was no point in riding tonight. He'd go early tomorrow.

His mind started in again on Grant. That hombre always traveled with a trio of gunmen, as if expecting to come under fire. Well, considering his tricky schemes, he was right to expect it. Yet he sure fooled the folks. They judged him an upright citizen, but he was twisty as a snake.

And he had sure bamboozled Midge. She would swear he was a straight shooter, a kind man, and she admired him. Yet this kind man was behind the death of her husband, the father of her child. Oh, Slade pointed the gun, but it was Grant's money that pulled the trig-

ger. Why did he do it. That was the puzzle. A man like
Grant, with so much to lose, wouldn't stick his neck out
unless there was profit in it. Did he need the stream that
bad after all? Maybe he wanted the Blake stream for the
future, for a big-time cattle herd. And just maybe there
was a secret prize hidden on the Blake land. He'd be
counting on Midge to sell. How long could Midge en-
dure the hardship of working the land by herself before
selling to Grant?

He mulled over it without satisfaction until a string
of curses from the nearby poker game made him turn to
the players. A heavyset cowboy with a stubble beard,
his face flushed with a drink, spoke in a harsh voice.
"Where the hell did you get that ace?"

He flung the insult at a neat gambler with a heavy
black mustache, who was wearing a black jacket, a
white shirt, and a string tie. He coughed gently, gazing
with mild astonishment at the husky cowboy. Then he
turned to the broad-shouldered player sitting to his right.
"That's one helluva question, don't you think, Wyatt?"

Wyatt's rugged face creased in a smile. "A man who
asks a question like that ain't foolin' around. He wants a
straight answer. So why don't you give it to him."

The gambler turned back to the cowboy. "That ace?"

"Yeah, that ace." The cowboy's voice was vicious
with threat.

"Came right outa the pack," the gambler said mildly.

The heavyset cowboy glared hard. "Not that pack,
mister. I don't how you did it, but you got the trickiest
fingers this side of hell."

The gambler in the black hat spoke calmly. "You got
a rough tongue, cowboy."

One of the players pulled at the cowboy's sleeve. "Take it easy, Chet. Don't do anything."

"Shut up," Chet hissed. "I just lost that pot because of that phony ace. I know a sharpshooter when I meet one." He stood slowly, his hand in a claw near his Colt .44.

The gambler was smiling, as if the last thing he had in mind was a gunfight. Mildly he asked, "Not listening to reason, Chet?"

"What?" Chet's hard face looked puzzled. In that moment the derringer appeared in the gambler's hand and fired, the bullet tearing through Chet's gut. He clapped his hand to his belly, stared wildly at the blood, amazed at what had happened, then slowly sank to his knees and fell face-down. He wriggled there, breathing harshly.

The barkeep signaled a couple of men. "Get him to Doc Jenkins." They lugged the heavy cowboy out the door.

The gambler in the black hat, whose derringer had disappeared, coughed gently. As he collected the money in the pot, he spoke in his mild voice. "The sight of an ace makes some men go crazy. An unfortunate interruption. Let's go on with the game."

A man at the bar standing next to Slocum shook his head and said in a slow voice, "Chet was one dumb ox."

"Why so?" asked Slocum.

The man looked at Slocum. "He tried a shootout with Doc Holliday. With Wyatt Earp sitting just alongside. That was dumb. Even if Doc did slip an ace, you let a man like that win."

Slocum fingered his chin and thought about it. Doc Holliday might hate to lose, but he didn't play crooked

cards. Slocum lit a cigarillo, then figured that he'd had
enough of the Alhambra Saloon. He'd spend the night at
the Cosmopolitan Hotel, and after breakfast in the
morning he'd ease back to Black Rock sometime tomorrow. He walked out into the soft night air and stepped
along the warped sidewalk toward the hotel.

On the way he passed a slender, sinewy man riding a
dusty black horse. The man had just come into town,
but Slocum didn't know him. Not by sight anyway. But
neither did Rudabaugh know Slocum by sight. They
glanced at each other without recognition and went their
ways, Slocum to the hotel, Rudabaugh to the Alhambra,
known hangout for Cassidy and Doc Holliday.

11

It was a sweltering day, and the Arizona earth baked under a fierce sun. At the Blake ranch, Charlie sweated through his shirt as he worked the horses, chopped wood, and fixed the barn door, among other chores.

When he was through, he stared at the land shimmering in the heat. It was rich land, nourished by a fine flowing stream, which sparkled in the sunlight. If Slocum was correct in his suspicions, Charlie thought, Grant wanted something here bad enough to get Tim killed. Deciding on a look-see, Charlie saddled a gelding in the corral and rode the terrain till sundown, but he could find nothing to justify Grant's interest, nothing that looked like a place to bury gold. Only the stream, which Grant's cattle already used. He was tired when he reached the ranch house. He swung off the gelding and looked north toward Grant's spread. His reason for being here was the hope that Grant might visit Midge. But no Grant.

He reached the ranch house feeling hungry and bleak.

For dinner Midge made chicken with biscuits, yams, and okra, putting him in mind of his childhood. "It was a rotten day for doing chores," she said, looking compassionately at his weary face.

"It was all right. I like the heat."

They didn't talk much; he was tired, and she seemed preoccupied.

Because Midge didn't care for smoking in the house, after he'd finished eating, Charlie went out to the porch to light up. The sky gleamed with millions of starry diamonds. And looming up against the horizon was the vast, humped profile of Mule Mountain. The summer scent of flowers floated on the breeze, and the howl of a lonely coyote made the night mournful.

Charlie Blake's thoughts drifted to Slocum, and he wondered what, if anything, he'd found in Tombstone.

He smoked his cigarillo to its last inch and scrunched it with his boot. Then the door creaked open and Midge stood there in a loose gingham dress. She looked at the sky. "A beautiful night." She sat in a chair on the porch and glanced at Charlie, who was lost in his thoughts.

"What are you thinking of, Charlie?"

He smiled. "Of the dinner. It put me in mind of the old days."

She smiled too. "When we were small fry?"

He laughed. "You were one helluva tomboy. Tough as nails. You kept the boys on the run. Now look at you."

She laughed. "I remember They were wild times. You and Tim were crazy buckeroos."

The mention of Tim sobered Charlie. He locked his hands behind his head and looked at the sky. "He's gone now. His life snuffed out by a mangy gunslinger."

Her face tightened, and she turned away.

"But at least," Charlie said, "he's not wiped off the face of the earth."

"What do you mean?"

"He's left a piece of himself, with you."

She looked hollow-eyed. "I'd rather not think about that."

Charlie bit his lip, feeling that he understood. Any reference to Tim touched a raw nerve, because her child would be born fatherless. A mournful future.

She changed the subject. "Tell me, Charlie. Why did Slocum run off to Tombstone? Seemed awful sudden."

He tensed. She had thrown a hot coal which he didn't know how to juggle. Midge admired the hell out of Grant; she'd be offended to learn they were still digging at that hole.

He hated lying and decided to pitch the truth. "I don't like to tell you this, Midge. But Slocum wanted to play one more chip before he closed down on Grant."

"What do you mean?" There was a harsh edge to her voice.

"He's gone to get the lowdown on Slade. What brought Slade from Tombstone to Black Rock? If he was a hired gunman."

She stared helplessly. "So, in spite of all I've said, you still go on, wanting to make a devil out of Mr. Grant." She hugged her body with both her arms, as if to warm herself against the cool of the evening. "All

right. Go on, do what you want. You won't find anything." Her voice became bitter. "What riles me is that,
of all men, Mr. Grant has been the kindest. Yet you
have made him the target of your suspicions and hate."

She stood up, opened the porch door, and went back
in the house.

She was aware that she was agitated, and that such a
mood wouldn't help the life growing inside her. She
went to her bedroom, where she hoped to find peace
and quiet. She lay down in the big bed, the one she had
shared with Tim. After he had been shot, she became
sharply aware of Tim's absence from the bed. It surprised her how quickly his memory had dimmed.

Her thoughts were focused elsewhere, mostly on the
child she was carrying. The very thought of the child
sent tingles of pleasure through her body. She felt in
tune with nature, and that nothing could give her more
happiness than to give birth to a male child. She visual-
ized him as a young boy, riding a colt alongside her
down the range. The picture in her mind gave her quick
comfort.

She lay quietly on the bed, looking through the window at the star-studded heavens. She thought of many
things. Of Slocum gone to Tombstone. Of Charlie hanging on in her ranch. Of Tim in his grave behind the
house. And of Grant on his big ranch, probably counting his cattle.

She realized that at a time like this, when she most
needed peace of mind for her baby, she seemed to get
nothing but trouble thrown at her. The shootings. And
the threat of more. She was sick of it. And it had come
to a head with the arrival of Slocum. Tim had sent for
Slocum, that's what really started it.

The weight in her body felt uncomfortable, and she turned to lie on her side.

She looked through her window at the big stars sparkling in the sky. She watched them for a while, then began to feel better.

Rudabaugh pushed through the doors of the Alhambra and strode to the bar. The smoke of tobacco and the smell of whiskey hit him.

The barkeep came up. "Howdy, Mr. Rudabaugh. What brings you to this rootin', shootin' town?"

"Nothin' good, Barney. Gimme some whiskey."

Barney brought out the good stuff and filled a glass, which Rudabaugh gulped down. Barney refilled it and watched Rudabaugh's dark eyes sweep the crowd. His gaze stopped on Kid Cassidy, who was sitting at the table with Marylou. He downed the second drink then walked to the Kid's table. The Kid looked at him, his good-looking face expressionless.

"Hello, Kid, I'm Rudabaugh. You remember me?"

"I remember."

"I'm here for Mr. Grant in Black Rock. Got a business proposition for you."

The Kid's light blue eyes were fixed calmly on Rudabaugh, who felt queasy. The Kid was the best gun in Tombstone, it was said, and you walked on eggs when you talked to him. And that damned girl, sitting there— she spoiled things, too.

"Say, Kid, can we talk private?"

The Kid glanced at Marylou, who looked coldly at Rudabaugh, then stood up and walked over to the bar. The Kid watched her, smiling.

"What's the job?" The Kid asked.

"Nuthin' dirty. A straight draw. You take on this hombre in a straight draw. He's a fast gun."

The Kid's voice was lazy. "Straight draw. Why?" His keen eyes studied Rudabaugh.

Rudabaugh cleared his throat. He didn't like to show Grant's secret hand, but it would be dangerous not to be truthful with the Kid. The same instinct that made him a great gunfighter helped him smell out deceit.

"Grant's been tryin' hard to get rid of this hombre for some time. He's too sharp to get bushwhacked. And he's plenty good. We've put a lot of gunmen on him. But he's still here. Grant wants him dead and figures only the best can do it. You or Doc Holliday. I reckon Doc doesn't need the money. He makes plenty with cards. So the job's yours if you want it."

The Kid's slate blue eyes gleamed. "Who is this hombre?"

"A man called Slocum." Rudabaugh paused to light up a cigar. "He's fast."

"They're all fast," the Kid's lips twisted sardonically.

"Oh, he's fast all right. He knocked off your pal Jim Slade."

The Kid looked startled, then thoughtful. "What's this Slocum look like?"

Rudabaugh shrugged. "Tell the truth, I've never seen him. Probably nothin' special. When you come to Black Rock, we'll point him out."

"He might be here in Tombstone right now."

Rudabaugh was jolted. "Here?"

"A man came in tonight," drawled the Kid. "He asked about Slade."

Rudabaugh frowned. "Asked what?"

"Wanted to know if Slade had been a gun for hire."

The Kid smiled slowly. "And who hired him."

Rudabaugh scowled. "What'd you tell him?"

"I told him you hired him for John Grant."

Rudabaugh digested that, then puffed at his cigar while he did some deep thinking. Who in hell would come to Tombstone and ask about Slade if not Slocum? Black Rock was only a three-hour ride from Tombstone. Well, if it was Slocum, he sure had hit the jackpot. He might learn that it had been Grant's fine hand behind the gunslinger assaults on him. That is, if Slocum could put it all together, which wouldn't be easy. After all, Slade was hired to get Tim Blake, not Slocum. It was Slocum who'd gone after Slade and beat him in the draw.

This Slocum had to be one heller with a gun. How else could he have come through Seth, Kirk, and finally Slade? All hot-shot gunslingers. Rudabaugh knew. He had hired them. Hired them for Grant. But he never knew why. When you worked for Grant, you didn't ask why, you just carried out orders. Still, it wasn't hard to figure that Grant wanted in the worse way to stop Slocum from getting to Black Rock.

But he had gotten there.

And Charlie Blake had gotten there too. Another thorn in Grant's side.

The Kid spoke coolly. "Do you reckon Slocum might go after Grant?"

Rudabaugh grinned. "He'd have to go through Hauser and two other top guns who stick closer to Grant than his underwear."

The Kid's blue eyes had a faraway look. He was thinking of Slocum, the hombre who had gone upstairs with Marylou. The Kid's first impulse had been to blast his balls off. But the man showed no fear, and the Kid liked that. Liked him even more as they talked. The Kid had faced a lot of desperate men looking into the abyss the moment before the draw, and he had seen the fear. He could sense the fiber of a man, and Slocum had it. Men like that were rare. It didn't surprise him that Slocum had beat Slade. How fast was Slocum? he wondered. Anyway, Slocum had what the Kid felt he had—the guts to challenge death without fear. No, it didn't appeal to the Kid to destroy a man like that. That's what the Kid was thinking when Rudabaugh spoke.

"So, Kid, what do you think? You call out Slocum. You know how—the wrong word, the insult. Then blast him. It gets you three hundred dollars. One fifty if you say yes, the rest when you pull your gun."

The Kid's eyes widened. Three hundred bucks. A fine piece of money. Suddenly, to his own surprise, he heard himself say, "Okay, I'll do it."

Later, when he thought about it, he realized it hadn't been the money. No, not the money. Mostly it had been the crying need to measure himself against the best. Slocum had beat Slade.

How good was he?

From the bar, Marylou watched Rudabaugh count out money. A helluva lot of money. She watched the Kid put it in his pocket and shake hands with the grinning Rudabaugh. As he passed the bar, he looked at her, and she hated the look in his eyes.

She strolled over to the Kid's table and sat down. The slate-blue eyes in his good-looking face were glittering with secret pleasure.

"I don't like Rudabaugh," she said.

He looked at her silently.

"And I don't like," she went on, "the job he offered you, whatever it is."

His face cracked in a grin. "But it's goin' to pay three hundred dollars."

Her eyes narrowed. "Must be mighty dangerous if it's that much money."

"It ain't."

"Who is it?" she asked.

His smile was sardonic. "The gent who had the brass balls to take you upstairs. Under my nose."

She was startled. "Slocum?"

"Yeah, Slocum." He paused. "Good thing I didn't pull my gun before. Now I get three hundred for doin' what I should've done for nothin'."

Marylou stared at him. This handsome young hunk with the lightning draw up against Slocum, a man she really cottoned to. A cold hand clutched at her heart. "Don't do it, Kid."

There was a long silence. Then he spoke in his lazy drawl. "I think I will do it. One, because you like that polecat. Two, because I like the money. Three, because I'm goin' to show him I'm the fastest gunfighter alive."

She stood up. "And four, because you're a blind young fool."

A light flashed in his eyes, and his hand moved like a streak.

The saloon was silent as she walked out, stiff and erect, her face showing the red imprint of his fingers.

That night, Slocum, deep in sleep, heard a sound, a scratch on his door. He came up, instinctively alert, and reached for his gun. He could see through the window that the moon had shifted in the sky. It had to be late. He came to his feet and moved silently to the door.

A whisper. "Slocum."

Marylou! He listened carefully for another sound. The Kid? Had he changed his mind and was using her as a decoy? No. The Kid wouldn't stoop to tricks. He'd come at you straight. She was alone.

Must be my sex appeal, he thought sardonically.

He slipped the door open. She came in, her pretty face somber, her lip swollen. He closed the door behind her and stared at her fat lip. "Run into a saloon door, Marylou?"

"No time for joking. Slocum, you've got an enemy in town."

His eyes narrowed.

"A man named Rudabaugh. He just paid the Kid to shoot you down."

Slocum was jolted. Rudabaugh, Grant's foreman. So he'd come to Tombstone to buy a top gun. He had done that to get Slade. That clinched it.

He looked at the pretty girl, who had turned to the window. She had come here, risking plenty. Her fat lip —the Kid's work, no doubt.

She turned and spoke slowly. "Why'd I come here? I want your promise to leave town. Before you meet the Kid. Get out now. I wouldn't like to see you hurt. And I don't want the Kid hurt either."

He sighed. Was there any point in running? If he went to Black Rock, the Kid would come there, too. Grant paid his gunslingers enough. He'd eat breakfast, and if the Kid didn't show, he'd leave.

"I'll leave early tomorrow, Marylou. Right now I need my sleep."

She was hit by the fear that Slocum might not be drawing breath by tomorrow. With a quick movement, she pulled her dress off and stood there, naked and beautiful, her mouth partly open. "Whatever happens, let me give you something."

She came toward him, her eyes glowing, her mind tingling with the excitement of making love with a man on the verge of death.

12

Grant smoked a cigar and looked out at his range. Within his view were hundreds of cattle, and in the shimmer of the heat they looked dreamlike. His gray eyes turned from the range to look down toward the Blake ranch. The stream that twisted through the Blake spread glinted brightly in the sun. His mind worked on the Blake ranch, and his jaw set hard. He turned to Hauser, one of his three bodyguards nearby. Hauser, aware that Grant wanted him, came forward.

Grant stared at Hauser, a gunfighter with his busted hook nose and narrow dark eyes. He liked Hauser because he was loyal. If he told Hauser to ride to hell and shoot the devil, damned if he wouldn't try.

"Hauser. Get Eddie Corne. I want to talk to him."

"Sure, boss."

Grant watched Hauser go toward the bunkhouse,

then turned to the corral, leaned against it, and watched one of his hands trying to break a wild bronc.

The bronc was rough and bucked madly, finally tossing the rider, who landed on his butt with a string of curses. It was a comic scene, but Grant didn't laugh. Though his eyes were on the bronc, his thoughts were far away.

Then he saw Eddie walking toward him with Hauser. Eddie walked with a casual gait that made Grant grind his teeth. He had placed Eddie and Terry at Midge's place to do a simple job: find the right moment off the ranch to bushwhack Slocum and Charlie Blake. It should have been easy as eating pie. What could be easier than to shoot polecats who didn't suspect you were after their hide? Yet they had screwed up. At least Terry had tried hard enough to get himself killed. But this mangy polecat continued to walk around after screwing up the job.

Eddie stood in front of Grant with bleary blue eyes and a hangdog look.

"Eddie," Grant said pleasantly, "how'd you happen to mess up that Slocum job? Shoulda been easy."

"It wasn't easy, Mr. Grant." Eddie spoke in calm, measured tones. "Somehow, Slocum smelled out we were tailing him. When we tried to gun him down he let loose. Shot the hell outa Terry. Missed me by a hair. He can shoot. I was lucky to get out with a whole skin."

Grant's voice was cold. "There's always an excuse for men who screw up. I'm not interested in excuses. I'm givin' you another shot. It's Charlie Blake. He's back on the Blake ranch. Get over there and stay outa sight. But get on his trail, and when it's right, then blast him to hell. Bury the body where nobody can find it."

He glared at Eddie. "Is that clear enough?"

"Yeah," Eddie said, but he stood still, trying to read Grant. He then glanced uncertainly at Hauser.

"Well?" said Grant. "What are you waitin' for? Get goin'."

"Yes, Mr. Grant. I won't screw up this time." He turned toward the bunkhouse.

"*There's* a strange breed of gunman," Grant said.

Hauser shrugged. "You can't always know, boss."

Grant and Hauser watched Eddie walking away. "After he does the job, put out his lamps. He knows too much." Grant looked at Hauser. "Are you clear, Hauser?"

Hauser laughed. "I'm clear, boss."

In Tombstone, Slocum dressed, checked his Colt, and walked out of the hotel into the street. He strolled toward the Maison Doree, an eating place. It was a clear day; in a cloudless sky the sun was climbing with the promise of heat. Cowboys lugged supplies from the merchandise store, men loafed on the porches, small boys played on the street.

Slocum went into the Maison Doree and sat at the window. There were five customers, who looked him over curiously. One, stubble-bearded, nodded, as if he knew him. A shapely, red-lipped young waitress with dark hair in bangs came over. "I'm Gigi. What would you like?"

I'd like you, Gigi, sometime, he thought, but aloud he said, "Gigi, you see a hungry man. I'll have steak and eggs, plenty of biscuits, and coffee."

"I like a hungry man," she said before leaving.

He glanced out the window. There was no sign of

Kid Cassidy, but that meant nothing. Last night, just before Marylou had slipped out of his bed, whispered, "If you leave town early, there may not be a showdown. I'll keep the Kid busy."

Slocum shrugged. That wasn't too likely. Kid Cassidy had been paid big money, she had said. It was surprising that he'd taken the job. He seemed friendly last night, but something had changed him. The money? That'd be disappointing. But money had corrupted bigger men than Kid Cassidy.

Gigi brought a big dish with steak and eggs, a plate of steaming biscuits, and a big cup of coffee. He dug in with gusto. After he finished, he sipped his coffee. So what about the Kid? Had Marylou stopped him? Men like Kid Cassidy were not stopped by women. She might delay him, but he'd come. If he took the money, he'd feel honor-bound to pull his gun. Slocum sipped his coffee reflectively.

Trouble was that Kid Cassidy was a very fast gun. Tension streaked through Slocum. He smiled. Was it fear? You never knew when it came to the moment of the draw. Anything could happen. If you felt fear, it could slow your reflexes just a whisker, enough to make you second best. Who but a mule wouldn't feel fear facing a lighting-fast gunslinger with a famous rep.

Gigi came up with her coffee pot, smiled, and refilled his cup. Though she wanted to talk, she said nothing because of what she saw in Slocum's eyes.

Slocum sipped the fresh coffee and thought about fear. The way you handled it was to realize there was no escape, that if you survived today, you might get hit tomorrow. Death was unbeatable. So why fear? Fear would not keep you alive for two moments longer. In fact, fear in a showdown got you killed faster. And it stripped you of your style. Slocum smiled. It didn't matter whether you won or lost in the game of life, because everyone lost—it was how you played the game.

Slocum sipped the fresh coffee and liked the warmth in his belly.

Then he saw Kid Cassidy. He was strolling in his easy way down Main Street toward the cafe. Slocum studied him. The Kid's gait was catlike, and he walked like a lord of death. Slocum had seen lots of gunfighters in his time, and he knew the dangerous ones. The Kid was one. Nature had designed him for gunfighting. Sinewy, not an ounce of fat, all muscle. It'd be a pity if the Kid was indeed looking for a draw.

The door opened and the Kid headed to his table. Whatever it was, Slocum would learn the truth, pretty damned quick.

"Mind if I sit, Slocum?" His voice was calm but his eyes were stony, like the eyes of someone who didn't want to connect with someone he expected to be dead.

"Sure, sit down."

Gigi came alongside."Bring me some coffee," he said. "I'm late starting today."

"Sorry to hear that," Slocum said, and he couldn't help but smile, thinking about Marylou.

"Yeah, I was up earlier, but Marylou started to get mighty busy. I did something I never do. Pushed her outa bed."

Slocum lit up a cigarillo. He wasn't sure the bedtime activities of the Kid interested him.

Kid Cassidy's rugged, handsome face leaned close. "You know, Slocum, yesterday, when you took

Marylou upstairs, without a damned look at me, I was achin' to put a bullet up your tail."

Slocum's mouth tightened. Kid Cassidy was going to unfold a story that had to have one sad end.

"But I took a shine to you. I figured you were my kind of fella." The Kid paused to sip his coffee. He put down his cup, and an edge came into his voice. "But I been thinkin' things over. And I realize you slighted me by takin' Marylou."

"Funny thing about a real woman, Kid," Slocum said, "She believes she doesn't belong to anyone."

"That's not my point of view."

They were silent as Gigi came to refill the coffee cups. They waited for her to leave. But other customers had their ears cocked, aware that something big might shortly be happening in Tombstone.

Kid Cassidy picked up his cup. "Another thing, Slocum. Looks like you somehow made a bad enemy of a powerful man. That wasn't smart. A man like that can buy a fast gun. Then where is Slocum?"

Slocum had to smile. "Kid, I like you. And I'd hate to tangle with you. Got no quarrel with you. I know you're fast. I respect that, and I'd like to leave it like that. We go our ways."

The Kid shook his head. "There's money in this. Plenty of money. It's not cheap to draw on you, Slocum." He stopped to put his cup down. "But it's not the money, it's something else."

Slocum was surprised, because he had thought it might be either Marylou or the money. But something else pushed Kid Cassidy. "What would that be, Kid?"

The Kid's good-looking face broke into a strange smile. "It was Slade. You say you beat Slade. Tell you

the truth. I thought Slade one of the best guns in Tombstone. I never was quite sure that even *I* could beat
Slade. And you say you did." He cleared his throat.
"That's why you and me are goin' to have a showdown
on that street in ten minutes." He paused. "After you
finish your breakfast. It's the least I can do."

Kid Cassidy stood up, grim-faced. "I'll be out
there."

One of the men at the cafe, who had recognized Slocum, went lickety-split out of the cafe and told folks
that he'd seen Slocum in a gunfight in Dodge City and
that he was greased lightnin'. And that he would have a
showdown with Kid Cassidy. The town all knew who *he*
was—the fastest gun in Tombstone.

Word went out like wildfire—to the saloon, to most
of the town. Soon all Tombstone knew the stuff that
makes legend was about to happen on Main Street.

The broad dirt street was empty, of course, except for
the fierce blaze of sunlight. To stay out of the reach of
gunfire, men pressed against doorways, huddled on
porches, lurked on rooftops, small fry burrowed in
spaces under buildings.

Though there was jubilation in Tombstone, behind it
was the somber realization that two men would be facing each other with death in their guns.

Slocum, still in the cafe, held an almost empty coffee
cup. The remaining customers watched him furtively.

Slocum didn't like what had happened. His showdown should be with Grant, not with Kid Cassidy. The
Kid, like Slade and all the others, were guns that he had
to go through to get to Grant. And he still didn't know
why Grant wanted him dead. But he'd never find out
unless he made it through Kid Cassidy. Slocum's jaw

hardened with anger because Grant, with his money, could put the Kid up to this.

But that was not entire truth, for the Kid had been jealous about Marylou. And he had to prove to himself he was top gun.

Slocum felt a wave of weariness. Over and over, he found himself facing young gunfighters trying to prove they were the best. He wondered what forced men to put their lives on the line, just to find out if they were faster.

He was facing that burden again. Kill or be killed.

Slocum took a deep breath, composed his mind, then stood up, adjusted his holster, walked to the door, and went out into the street.

The customers let out a long sigh, aware that a drama of death was about to be played. Everyone went to the door to peer out.

Slocum looked down the street. It was empty, baking in a fierce sun, with ramshackle houses on either side. Far down at the other end, a lone, lithe figure leaned against the side pillar of the saloon, waiting in the shadow. Slocum figured he'd walk halfway; by then, Kid Cassidy would detach from the saloon, move to the center of the street, and wait, in the gunman's crouch.

Slocum started his walk, his mind ice-cool, his body mobilized.

Rudabaugh had got himself a front-row seat for the showdown by sneaking into the second story of an abandoned house on the street. From the closed window he watched Slocum walk in the hot sun: lean, powerful, invincible. Until this moment, Rudabaugh had felt the fight had a foregone finish—Kid Cassidy was an unbeatable gunfighter. Now he had a premonition of the Kid's defeat; he felt it in his bones. Slocum had beat every top gun thrown against him, and suddenly Rudabaugh felt that Slocum would beat Cassidy, too. You couldn't beat Slocum in a straight draw. A shiver of excitement passed through Rudabaugh. From this window, if he raised it a bit, he'd have a shot. Slocum would be dead in seconds, and nobody would know who or what had hit him. And think of the deal: he'd tell Grant that *he* did the killing. Make the boss grateful. And he'd pocket the extra $150 meant for Cassidy. Tell the Kid his life had been saved. That since Slocum had been killed by an unknown gun, he couldn't in fairness to Grant give the Kid the other $150. What a feather in his cap. Already Rudabaugh's pulse was pounding with excitement. He had to move fast. Slocum had reached a point parallel to the house. He'd have to shoot now. Nervously he grabbed his gun and reached for the window. It was too low, and he had to raise it. He tugged, but it stuck and scraped against the wood—a soft rasp of sound, not loud enough, he felt, to be heard outside. He stooped and thrust the barrel of the gun out of the window, where it caught the sudden gleam of sun. He saw Slocum's move in a blur, and the next instant Rudabaugh knew nothing, for a bullet had spattered his brains on the back walls. Rudabaugh's trigger finger, in reflex, fired wildly; he flopped back, his body twitching crazily for a few moments in a bloody heap on the floor.

Down on the street, folks were electrified at Slocum's lightning move. He had been too far from the Kid for it to be a showdown. They knew some low yellow dog had tried to ambush Slade. Whoever it was, folks hated him because he had tried to botch what they felt would be a great showdown between two top guns.

One of the customers standing with Barney, the bar-keep, outside the saloon, growled, "What the hell was that?"

"Some yellowbelly tried to shoot Slocum from the old Baines house," said Barney. "Did you see his move? He sure got the bastard."

"What about the showdown?

Barney studied Slocum. "It goes on."

Slocum, whose senses at a time like this were high-wired, had picked up the scrape of sound, the gleam of a gun barrel. He had walked gauntlets before and ex-pected everything. The split-second move of his gun had been automatic; whoever was up there was dead.

Now he glanced at Cassidy, still against the side of the saloon. Slocum put his gun back into its holster and again started his walk.

Kid Cassidy, with eagle eyes, had seen Slocum's sudden move and he had heard the two shots. Who the hell had it been? Rudabaugh, he was sure. He was dead too.

Cassidy had seen a lightning draw, the same draw that probably beat Slade. The Kid felt a strange quiver in his chest. He'd never felt anything like it before, and realized this was death fear, a loss of nerve. Until now, he had never met a gunman who touched his confi-dence. Slocum had done it. But there was nothing to do but go on. Tombstone was watching; he couldn't stop. He'd rather be dead than live in disgrace. He strolled toward the middle of the street and paused. His mind churned. It was stupid to freeze. He had never met a draw as fast as his. He had given men a three-second leeway—watched them go for their guns before he drew. Most gunfighters against him didn't even clear leather. So why worry? A smile came to his lips; he felt the old confidence. He moved again in his catlike gait, and when he reached the right position he stopped, his right hand near his holster. Then he thought of Marylou, he thought of money, he thought of himself: the best gunfighter of them all. He had to be—if not, then the hell with everything.

He watched Slocum coming. Slocum looked easy, not angry, just concentrated. Suddenly the Kid felt sorry, sorry that he hadn't taken Slocum's peace offer, sorry that he'd sold himself for money, sorry that he was ready to stick his head in the cannon's mouth for glory.

It was too late.

Slocum had stopped.

They watched each other.

The sun beat down fiercely. It was unbearable.

The Kid went for his gun and felt great. It was the old move, the lightning streak that nobody could beat.

Barney, at the Alhambra, had seen the showdown. He had had the best view, and he was telling it to a new customer, who had just ridden into town and wanted the details.

"Never saw a showdown like that, pardner," said Barney," and I been lookin' at 'em for twenty-odd years. Both fighters were like greased lightnin'. Slocum's walkin' down the street, the sun is beatin' down to fry an egg, then suddenly some sniper tries to hit Slocum from the old Baines place. And all of us waitin', holdin' our breaths, tryin' to guess who was the faster gun—the Kid or Slocum. We sure cussed that sniper out. But he never got his shot off. He stuck his gun out the window and Slocum's shooter come out like a blue streak. He fires. He puts his gun back in the holster. Now Slocum starts again, walkin' down the street. He stops. The Kid comes out from the shadow. They're standing in the middle of the empty street, nothin' moving, just the sun fryin' the street. Then they went for their guns."

Barney paused and lifted a beer that he had drawn for himself.

The customer glared. "What the hell happened?"

Barney leaned toward him and whispered, "They both got hit. They staggered." He paused dramatically. "But where were they hit? Well, they weren't really hit, they were nicked—in the shoulder and the arm. Something of a wonder. You see, pardner, neither of them went for the kill. You want the reason? They liked each other. Didn't want a kill. So that's the way it ended. Both nicked. What did it prove? Each gun was fast as the other. So that was it."

Barney smiled. "Slocum left Tombstone right away. Had unfinished business in Black Rock, he said. We found Rudabaugh, that yellowbelly, up in the old Baines house. At the window. His head was blown to pieces. That's how it goes, pardner. Another whiskey?"

13

Charlie Blake rode out of the sun into a stand of cotton-woods where a man could find cool shade. He swung off his horse, took his canteen from the saddlebag, raised it to his lips, then froze as he heard his name called softly.

"Charlie."

With a sinking feeling, he recognized the voice and was about to go for his holster, when he heard the voice again.

"No guns, Charlie, no guns!"

Something in Eddie's voice made him believe, so he stopped and looked.

Eddie Corne came out of the dense brush, his hands outstretched, showing no gun. Astonished, Charlie stared at him. Short, robust, his face flushed, as if he'd been drinking, his blue eyes anxious, his mouth twisted in a half smile. Charlie stayed alert, ready to go for his gun, puzzled by Eddie's presence on the Blake ranch.

"You got to be crazy to come here."

Eddie came forward, showing good intent by keeping his hands far from his holster. "Got somethin' important to tell you, Charlie."

"Tell me this, you bastard. Why'd you try to bush-whack me and Slocum?"

Eddie looked at him silently. Finally he spoke. "Listen, Charlie, Mr. Grant is no friend to you or Slocum. Know that?"

Charlie watched him closely. That was true, but why was he telling it. What kind of trick was this?

"Grant would like you and Slocum dead," Eddie said.

Charlie's teeth clenched and his hand moved closer to his gun. This had to be a trick. Did Eddie have a sidekick lurking in the bushes? "What the hell's goin' on? What are you doin' on this land?"

Eddie showed his palms. "Been sent by Grant to kill you, Charlie."

Charlie was stunned. At any moment he expected a bullet to thud into his body from a gunman lurking in the brush. But nothing happened.

"Why tell me all this, Eddie?"

"I've got friends who tell me things. Grant sent Steele to kill Slade 'cause he knew too much. Now he's sent Hauser and his two coyotes, Burt and Tom, to shut me up." Eddie's face twisted. "Grant likes to keep a clean rep."

"That's why you're here?"

"Yes. I've got a bad feeling I'm not goin' to make a clean getaway. So I figured the way I could hurt Grant was to tell Slocum what I know. Where is Slocum?"

"Should be back from Tombstone sometime today."

"Tombstone?" Eddie looked thoughtful. "Grant sent Rudabaugh there to buy a fast gun."

"Like who?"

"I don't know. Could be Kid Cassidy."

Charlie was jolted. What if that did happen? Kid Cassidy was one of the best gunfighters in the territory. Suddenly he feared for Slocum.

Eddie pulled a cigarillo from his shirt pocket and lit it. "I hope for your sake that Slocum comes through. He's the only gun who can turn things around here." He puffed his cigarillo. "Grant has wanted Slocum out of the way for a long time. Did you know? Rudabaugh's been hirin' fast gunslingers to do that job."

Charlie stared at him. "Why in hell does Grant want Slocum dead?"

Eddie shook his head. "There's a reason. And it's on this ranch, that's where the reason is. Grant tries to keep his secrets."

He does that, Charlie thought. "So you think Hauser and his gunslingers are comin' after you?"

"I *know* it." Eddie's jaw muscles tightened as he snuffed the cigarillo. "I'm goin' now." He paused, then looked fixedly at Charlie. "If I were you, I wouldn't trust *anyone* that Grant knows." He walked toward the dense brush where he'd picketed his horse.

Charlie watched him. What in hell did he mean— don't trust anyone Grant knows? The phrase burned in his mind. Then he shook his head. It didn't make sense.

He went toward his horse, swung over the saddle, and started back toward the ranch house.

• • •

Eddie walked past staghorn sumac patches of violets, beds of daisies; he could smell the fresh scents of summer flowers. The sun rode bright in a blue sky, offering a clear view of the mountain range. It looked like a great day to be alive, but Eddie had bad premonitions.

He swung onto his horse and rode west, in a hurry to reach the trail to Tombstone. The trick was to get to Tombstone, find Slocum and his protecting gun. But Slocum might be dead as a doornail. Especially after a showdown with Kid Cassidy. Well, he'd just hope for the best.

He came out of the dense brush and rode north on the trail to Tombstone. He began to feel hopeful and was approaching the bend when they rode out from behind the massive cliff, the three of them, Hauser in front, his face masklike.

They reined up when they reached him. "'Lo, Eddie," Hauser said.

Eddie nodded.

Hauser swung down from his saddle. "Let's gab for a coupla minutes, Eddie."

"Sure," Eddie came down off his horse. The other two gunmen, Tom and Burt, also swung down from their horses. They were smiling.

Hauser studied Eddie's flushed face. "Hittin' the bottle pretty early."

"Had a few."

"Where were you headin', Eddie?"

"Tombstone."

"Tombstone?" Hauser turned to his men. "What do you think of that, Burt?"

Burt just kept smiling. Then he spoke in a comic drawl. "Did he say he was headed for *a tombstone*?"

They all laughed but Eddie. His flesh crawled. They had been on his trail to the Blake ranch, then had taken a shortcut to stop him at this crossing. He was locked in with three killers, and he could see no way out.

Hauser smiled slowly. "You got a lousy sense of humor, Eddie."

"What the hell do you want, Hauser?" Eddie said.

"What do I want? What Grant wants. A little killin'. Like Charlie Blake. Reckon you just did your job."

"Reckon," Eddie said.

"Blake is out then?"

"Dead out," said Eddie, and he started for his horse.

"You're a liar, Eddie." Hauser's voice was icy. And he waited.

Eddie stopped and felt his skin tingle. Hauser wanted him to draw, and that'd be certain death. Slowly he half turned. "If you think so, Hauser. A man's entitled to his opinion."

"You goin' to take that?" Hauser looked surprised.

"Sure." Eddie started again toward his horse.

"Hey." Hauser's voice grated. "Pull your gun or I'll shoot you down like a mangy mutt."

Eddie realized there was no escape. He turned slowly. They were three, but he'd never get past Hauser. He took a deep breath and went for his gun. He got it out of the holster, got the gun up, but Hauser had already fired. Eddie fell back, his fingers still holding the gun, and tried to shoot, but his fingers had no strength. He lay there, cursing softly.

"What'd you say, Eddie?" Hauser asked with mock concern.

Eddie's face was pale, and he spoke slowly. "Slocum will chop you to pieces, Hauser."

Hauser, in a sudden fury, fired three more bullets into Eddie's body.

"Thanks, you bastard," Eddie managed to say. "I hate a slow death."

His eyes closed.

The sun had almost hit the horizon, and the sky was a great stretch of primrose, orange, and crimson when Slocum reached the outskirts of the Blake ranch. He pulled up to look at the stony peaks catching the flaming light. Then he saw three buzzards flying in a circle, an unpleasant omen. He rode another fifty yards, scanning the land as he always did, and to his surprise saw Charlie camped near a cottonwood, with a coffeepot over the fire.

He rode toward him.

Charlie was smiling broadly. "Damn, I'm glad to see you, Slocum."

Slocum frowned. "Did you have doubts?"

"Plenty. I heard that Kid Cassidy might have a gun out for you."

Slocum was astonished. He had left Tombstone immediately after the showdown. "How in hell would you know that?"

"Damn!" Charlie's eyes grew big. "You did. You had a showdown with the Kid."

"I did." Slocum looked somber. "But how did you know?"

Charlie ignored the question. "You beat the Kid? Tell me that first."

"No. It was a standoff." Slocum touched his shoulder gently. "Now tell me. It's hard to believe news could get here that fast."

"You won't believe this, Slocum. Eddie Corne, you know him. Grant's hired gun who worked here, who tried to ambush us—he came here and told me."

"Eddie?" Slocum repeated it in wonder.

"That one. He said Grant ordered him to shoot me." Charlie grinned. "He didn't do it because he learned that Hauser had orders to kill *him* after he did it." Charlie paused. "Seems like Eddie knows too much, and Grant wanted him shut up."

It figured, Slocum thought. Grant was one rotten dog who killed his own people. Slocum loosened his red neckerchief and mopped his face. "Well, if Eddie came to kill you and didn't, it means someone else is going to come and try again. Like Hauser. Right?"

"We should be ready," Charlie said grimly.

They were silent for a moment, looking at the high, scarred crags nearby.

Then Charlie turned to Slocum. "Another thing Eddie said—Rudabaugh has been hiring gunslingers to put you to rest."

Slocum looked grim. After the showdown, he'd gone back to the Baines house to see who had tried the sneaky gun trick and found Rudabaugh in a bloody mess. "Rudabaugh won't do that anymore."

Charlie stared. "Finished?"

Slocum nodded. "Did Eddie say why Grant wants me dead?"

"He said that the reason was on this ranch, whatever it is."

"On this ranch," Slocum repeated.

"Yeah. Eddie said one other thing before he went." Charlie spoke slowly. "He said not to trust anyone Grant knows."

Slocum's brows knitted. "Eddie knows a lot, where the hell is he?"

Charlie pointed up. "I been watchin' those buzzards."

Slocum sighed "We may have to cross Eddie off."

"So what happened in Tombstone? Get some answers?"

"Yeah, from Cassidy himself. Rudabaugh hired Slade to kill Tim Blake." He paused. "And behind Rudabaugh was Grant."

There was a long silence.

Charlie turned to look in the direction of the ranch house, miles away. Slocum looked too. "Where's Midge?" he asked.

"Home, I reckon." Charlie's blue eyes looked hazy. "Doesn't it seem strange that Eddie should say the reason why Grant is doing all this killing is right on this ranch?"

"On this ranch?" Slocum stroked his chin. "It's not the stream, he doesn't need that. He gets the water free. It's not gold, there isn't any. Only one thing left."

Charlie watched him, as if hypnotized.

"And that's Midge," Slocum said finally.

There, it was finally spoken, the unmentionable. Was Midge somehow tangled up with Grant?

There was a long silence. It always seemed strange to Slocum that whenever the trail led to Grant, Midge would say it was wrong. She argued that he was straight. Yet Grant had been crooked as a dog's hind leg. Had she'd been protecting him? That could only mean there was something between them.

Slocum spoke slowly. "Can we really believe Midge is in on this? After all, she's carrying Tim's kid. Would she want the father of her kid to be dead? I don't know, Charlie. It doesn't make sense."

The two men were silent, thinking.

The three gunmen looked down at Eddie's bullet-ridden body: hook-nosed Hauser, smiling, blue-eyed Burt, and Tom, a sturdy gunslinger with a weathered face.

Hauser said thoughtfully, "What a waste."

"What do you mean?" asked Burt, smiling as usual.

"He saw it coming and took it like a man," Hauser said. "He had balls."

"A gritty little guy," said Burt.

Hauser, whose nerves were taut after shooting, stared at him. "What are you smilin' about, Burt?"

Burt's look didn't change. "What's wrong with it?"

"Just shot the hell outa Eddie, one of our boys. Not exactly the right thing to do, and you're still smiling."

Burt tried to rearrange his face, but it didn't work. "I don't know, Hauser. Reckon it's my natural look."

"Burt would smile if you boiled him in oil. That's how he is," said Tom.

"Reckon it's better than cryin'." Hauser went to his saddlebag, pulled out a bottle of whiskey, took a long haul, then passed it to Burt. "What the hell was all that he said about Slocum?"

Burt held the bottle in his hand. "A lotta crap. Slocum's dead as a doorknob right now." He took a haul from the bottle and passed it to Tom.

"Sure," Tom drawled. "Cassidy could give Slocum lessons in the fast draw." He drank and passed the bottle back to Hauser, who looked serious.

"There's something funny about Slocum. Rudabaugh told me he hired some real sharp guns and sent them to

Bitter Creek and to Red River to knock off Slocum. But still that hombre shows up in Black Rock. How'd that happen?"

"Maybe those pistoleers just took the money and run for the border," Tom suggested.

Hauser shook his head. "Not likely. Rudabaugh wouldn't hire a bad gun. Not him." He stared at Eddie's body. "Bury him."

The men got out their shovels and started to dig.

"Rudabaugh should be back from Tombstone by now." Hauser took off his short flat hat and mopped his brow. "It's a rotten hot day."

Burt stopped digging. "Do you reckon Eddie did his job on Charlie Blake?"

Hauser froze. "What the hell does that mean?"

Burt looked surprised. "I mean you called Eddie a liar."

Hauser looked with pity at Burt. "You call a man a liar, you force him to draw. That's why I did it. As for Charlie, it wouldn't take much to knock off a varmint like him." He watched them smooth the dirt over the grave. "Well, let's go back to the ranch. Grant will be glad to hear Eddie's pushin' daisies."

John Grant came out on the porch of his big house and took a long drink of Scotch whiskey sent him from St. Louis. It tasted good and felt good in his gut; it was good stuff, not the rotgut they sold in the saloons. Grant had a fear of saloon whiskey, which a peddler once told him was made from raw alcohol, creosote, liquid coffee for color, and chewing tobacco for extra bite. No wonder the saloon leeches crashed from gut trouble, if they didn't go loco first and begin to shoot the chandelier.

The sun was sinking on the horizon, and the sky was all ablaze, a great time of day. It was when he liked to look at the raw-backed mountains, at his vast land with its endless herds.

Yes, he sure had a hell of a lot of material things, but he didn't have anyone to leave it to after he passed on.

His first wife, Matilda, had died in childbirth, taking along the baby, a boy. One of his great tragedies—Matilda, a beautiful young girl, and the son he hungered for.

After that body blow, he had sunk himself in work, buying and selling cattle, building a fortune. But the time came when he stopped to question himself. Why in hell was he building all this? It was crazy.

He had no heir, and no woman who interested him.

That's when he first took notice of the Blakes. He wanted the stream on their land and rode down to make an offer—and got a good look at Midge, a buxom, violet-eyed honey with a hell of a spirit. She had to have a lot of fire in that body.

He made a generous offer to Tim Blake, which Tim had declined. "Use the water," Tim said, "just as you're doing, Mr. Grant. God didn't put down the stream for one man's use."

Grant was amused. Mighty generous, but the man was a fool. A stream in the West was a gold mine—you had to have water for your animals and your land. This Tim Blake, like a tenderfoot, just didn't know.

But what fascinated Grant was the light, flashing eyes of Midge Grant. She had to be too much of a woman for Tim.

She was. One day, when Tim Blake had gone off on business to Phoenix, Midge washed her hair, bathed, dressed in her best bib and tucker, and rode out alone to the Grant ranch.

That started the thing between them. Grant thought of the days that followed, and his eyes glowed. Now he had a woman and something else.

But Tim Blake stood like a curse between him and what he wanted. And scandal was one thing Grant hated. He had a fine clean rep in the territory and was jealous of it.

He took another haul of the liquor, then saw the three riders coming from the west. That would be Hauser and his boys. Grant's smile was cold. It should mean Eddie Corne and Charlie Blake had turned up their toes. And when Rudabaugh came in, it would mean Slocum had joined them.

Grant felt the nice tingle he always got when his plans jelled. He thought of what his men had to do and his face darkened. It was a tough life. He hadn't become a cattle king by playing tiddlywinks. It took tough decisions, a lot of blood, and some crafty tricks.

That's how you made it in this big country where you matched your wits against wits, guts against guts, man against man.

Hauser came riding up and lifted from his saddle. His voice was polite. "Took good care of Eddie Corne, Mr. Grant."

Grant smiled. "Gave him a fine sendoff?"

"Yessir."

"After he did Charlie Blake?"

"Yessir. That's what he said."

Grant stared at him "Said? You checked, didn't you?"

Hauser flushed. "I figured he wouldn't lie about something like that."

Grant's voice was icy. "You figured? Don't 'figure', Hauser, ever. Make sure."

"Couldn't go ridin' in there with no excuse, sir. Especially after a killin'. We're trying to be mighty careful around Mrs. Blake."

Grant scowled. "Go over and find out what's what. I don't want guessing. That's how I do business."

"Want all of us to go, or just me?"

Grant shook his head. "Do you need three men to find out if Charlie Blake's dead?"

Hauser flushed. "I'll ride over." He told Tom and Burt to stay put, that he was going to check on Charlie Blake. As he rode, he cursed. Why did that sonofabitch Grant always make him feel stupid?

And Grant, watching him ride, thought that if he had to depend on men like Hauser, he'd land in the manure.

For that matter, Rudabaugh hadn't been that smart either. Not one gunslinger he hired could tumble that bastard Slocum. He had to put out big money to buy Kid Cassidy to do the trick. And think of the luck, that Slocum had gone to Tombstone. To find out about Slade, of course. What had put Slocum on that scent? Grant wondered. A lot of dirty laundry could tumble out. But it didn't matter, because Kid Cassidy's fast gun would put Slocum where he belonged.

But where the hell was Rudabaugh. He was overdue.

Then he saw the rider on a horse running all stretched out. A shiver of fear went through him.

The rider flung off his horse and walked up to Grant.

He brought his hand to his hat and stared hard.

"I'm Roy Smith, just rode in from Tombstone. Got news for you from Kid Cassidy."

Grant stared at the sweaty rider. "What is it, cowboy?"

"Cassidy says to tell you that Rudabaugh tried to ambush Slocum and got his head shot off."

Grant froze. That stupid sonofabitch Rudabaugh! Tried to grab some ready cash. Greedy little toad. So he cashed in his chips instead. But the showdown with Slocum, what about that?

"Cassidy told you this?" he growled. "What else happened?"

Roy Smith again looked curiously at Grant. "He said that he had a showdown with Slocum. That it was a standoff. Both men were wounded, nobody died."

Grant grimaced. Slocum! Still not dead. The guy was like a dagger in his heart.

"What kind of wound does Slocum have?"

"Don't know. I wasn't there. Don't think it was bad." The cowboy cleared his throat. "Cassidy'd like to get the rest of his money promised him. You're to give it to me. A hundred and fifty dollars."

The rest! Grant was furious." The deal was to kill Slocum, not wound him."

Roy Smith smiled slowly. "Well, that's how it worked out. They shot at each other and that's what happened. And I ain't one to argue with Kid Cassidy."

Though there was black anger in Grant's heart, he, too, didn't want to argue with Kid Cassidy. He'd give this insolent polecat the money and then figure out how to handle Slocum. Because if he wasn't hurt bad, he'd be on his way here. For a different showdown. Grant's teeth were on edge. He'd get ready. Hauser had gone to the Blake ranch. He'd go too. He had to talk to Midge. And he'd have to be careful. You never knew what you could run into.

From the scarred crags near the Blake ranch, Hauser saw the horses, then the two men talking. Charlie Blake alive! Damn. So Eddie Corne was a low-down, lyin' hyena. Well, he was finished, it didn't matter anymore.

Then Hauser recognized Slocum. Back from Tombstone—and not dead either. Did that mean he outdrew Kid Cassidy? Naw, he couldn't be that good. They just never had a showdown.

So what to do about Charlie Blake? Damn, he couldn't go back and tell Mr. Grant that Charlie was still breathing. "Why in hell didn't you stop him breathing, you were there?" That's what Mr. Grant would say, And he'd be right. There was Charlie down there, and Slocum with him. Not a bad shot from here. He just needed to get better clearance for his gun.

Slocum was facing north, and with his instinct for danger, he picked up a move on the scarred crags. His keen eyes, beneath the brim of his hat, stayed on it, and his body tensed. He spoke quietly. "I'll shoot in a moment, Charlie. We've got Hauser crawling on the high rocks with his gun. Come to make sure you're dead. He's angling for a clear shot. Drop now."

Charlie went flat as Slocum's gun, in a lightning move, barked.

The bullet split Hauser's head like a melon.

14

The sun had descended in the sky by the time Slocum and Charlie reached the Blake ranch house. Midge came to see them from the bedroom where she'd been lying down. She looked more pregnant than ever. She didn't smile. "Will you have something?"

"Whiskey might do," Slocum said.

"Might have some myself." She took a dark bottle off the shelf and filled three shot glasses. They drank. She poured another. "I feel like liquor." She drank half the glass. Looking at Slocum with a queer smile, she asked, "Where you been?"

"Tombstone."

"Terrible town. So many killings." Her voice was cool.

"Lotta killings in Black Rock, too," Charlie said, thinking of Tim.

She stroked her belly, protectively. "Hope my baby grows up in a gentler country."

Slocum squinted at her. What the hell was the truth about this woman? "Listen, Midge, I've got the low-down on Grant. He's not the man you think he is."

She looked down at her glass, as if she didn't want to hear it.

"He hired Slade's gun," Slocum said. "He sent Rudabaugh to Tombstone to hire Slade. A notorious gun-fighter. To quarrel with Tim. To force a showdown and kill him."

"You believe that?" The strange smile came to her lips again.

"I believe it."

"How do you know?"

"Kid Cassidy told me. He was there when Slade was hired."

She put her hands on her belly, as if whatever happened she would protect that child. "What now?"

Slocum's jaw hardened. "What do you suppose? Grant has got to pay."

A curious gleam came to her violet eyes. "Grant is a powerful man."

Slocum lit a cigarillo and puffed it. She seemed to take Grant's guilt cool as ice. "A bullet doesn't know who's powerful. What gets me is why he did it."

Charlie, his face flushed, had been studying Midge. "You've been takin' all this mighty easy. Most women would be screaming for his head. That's strange."

She just looked at him defiantly, a lovely-looking woman. Still silent. She raised her glass.

Charlie stayed on it, his eyes boring into hers, his voice rough. "You were tired of Tim, weren't you,

Midge? Tired of him. And Grant was nearby and rich."

Slocum turned to him.

"Oh yeah," Charlie said. "Tim wrote, told me that Midge didn't seem to be happy. Not the Midge we used to know."

Her lips curved in her strange smile, and she leaned close to Charlie. "No, I wasn't. But that's because Tim wasn't the man I used to know either."

"What's that mean?" demanded Charlie.

"I'll tell you." She drank more whiskey and her voice grated. "Tim wasn't a man."

They stared at her.

"Not anymore," she said. "He was wounded in the war, you remember. In the groin." She looked at them boldly. "It came on slow, this bad physical thing. Ruined him. That bedroom was a hellhole. I didn't know about such things. Not till it was too late. We were married, for better or worse. It couldn't be worse. Never should have married. And I always wanted a baby. I had to have a baby."

They stared at her.

"But you did get pregnant," Charlie finally said.

"Yes," she said calmly.

"But it's not Tim's kid," Slocum said.

"No," she said.

There was a long silence.

Charlie's eyes blazed. "So you cheated Tim, my brother, with that mangy dog Grant."

"I wanted a child. I needed a child. And Tim couldn't give me one." Her voice was harsh.

Charlie wasn't listening. "And Grant screwing the ass off you. He couldn't stand having Tim around and had him killed."

She shrugged. "Tim was dead anyway."

"You bitch," Charlie said and pulled his gun.

"Don't," said Slocum.

"She cheated my brother. And killed him," Charlie said, grim-faced.

A shot rang out, and Charlie turned to the window, saw Grant, and fell.

Grant came through the window, his face hard, holding his gun on Slocum, whose hand was at his holster. Grant glanced down at Charlie, bent double, barely alive, looking up at him. A smile twisted Grant's lips. "You can't shoot a pregnant woman, mister. Not in my territory. And certainly not someone carrying my kid."

He turned to Slocum. "Your gun, mister. And do it careful, by its handle. You're too dangerous to be alive."

Slocum took out his gun and tossed it on the floor.

Grant smiled. "In the end, I've got the winning card," he said.

There was silence.

Slocum's green eyes glowed. "One thing I'd like to know, Grant. Why'd you put those gunmen on me?"

Grant laughed. "Oh, we knew all about you, Slocum. Tim told us about your gun—best he'd ever seen. And I respected Tim's opinion. When Midge told me he'd sent for you, we figured it best to stop you before you got here, opened the can of worms, and started to use that gun. That's why I tried to stop you." His mouth hardened. "But you were too good. Till now."

"Why'd you kill Tim? They could have divorced."

Grant shook his head sadly. "He wouldn't have it. Hated my guts. Not that I blame him."

He pulled out a cigar, lit it, enjoying himself. "But I'll tell you the truth, Slocum. It's easy now—be all over for you in a couple of minutes."

He poured some whiskey, his eyes sharp on Slocum. "It wasn't *me* that wanted Tim dead. It was gentle Midge there. Her idea. She said he'd never let her go. You see, Slocum, she wanted a kid, and was ready for everyone to go down just to get one." He laughed. "Looks gentle as a doe, but she's a tiger."

It was true, Slocum thought, looking at her lovely, almost fragile features, her violet eyes—all a mask.

So that was it. For the sake of a kid she had cheated her husband, had him murdered, seduced her neighbor, Grant. At least four gunmen were dead. Also Slade, Steele, and Hauser were dead. Charlie, listening to all this, was dying, and he, Slocum, would shortly be dead.

Grant was looking at him with hard eyes. "You were more dangerous than Tim said. Can't afford to have you breathin', mister." He started to bring his gun up to fire at Slocum.

The shot came from the floor, where Charlie, who had been listening with closed eyes, feeling near death, managed with tremendous effort to raise his gun just enough. Grant hurtled back, red blood gushing from his chest. His eyes looked wild as he fell. "Damn it all! Damn her!" he croaked as he lay there dying.

Midge, in shock, came frantically to her feet, ran toward him, and, stumbling over Charlie's leg, hit against the table edge and fell. She groaned, and her hands went to her belly.

Then she screamed.

Five days later, Slocum had put his last things in the saddlebag, while the roan stood chafing, yearning for the trail.

Slocum went back for the last time into Doc Smith's house, where Charlie lay, a thick bandage around his midsection. For two days, after a big loss of blood, he'd hung near death. But with the bullet out, he'd come back from the edge.

Doc Smith smiled at Slocum. "He's goin' to make it."

Slocum looked down at Charlie's blue-eyed, craggy face and reached fondly for his hand. "You're a good man, Charlie Blake," he said. "And I'll see you in Tucson in a month. You'll be mended by then."

And so he bid him farewell, went out to the roan, and with a deep breath, swung over the horse and started to ride out of town, thinking.

A lot of blood had flowed since he had come to Black Rock to help Tim, a friend in trouble.

And the woman, Midge Blake, who started it all for the sake of a kid, had lost the kid in miscarriage. It had been a rough time for her, but Midge, at the Blake ranch, was still alive. But with memories like hers, perhaps it would be better if she weren't.

The sun rising in the east sent streaks of flaming orange and primrose over the big sky. The dawn of a new day.

The roan, high-spirited, feeling the joy of being on the trail, began to canter, rarin' to tear loose.

Slocum felt its joy, the joy of being alive.

He put the roan into a fast run toward the horizon.